BEAT ROUTE

BEAT ROUTE

WINSTON MANTON

authorHOUSE®

AuthorHouse™
1663 Liberty Drive
Bloomington, IN 47403
www.authorhouse.com
Phone: 1-800-839-8640

© *2011 by Winston Manton. All rights reserved.*

No part of this book may be reproduced, stored in a retrieval system, or transmitted by any means without the written permission of the author.

First published by AuthorHouse   07/26/2011

ISBN: 978-1-4567-8848-3 (sc)

Printed in the United States of America

Any people depicted in stock imagery provided by Thinkstock are models, and such images are being used for illustrative purposes only.
Certain stock imagery © Thinkstock.

This book is printed on acid-free paper.

Because of the dynamic nature of the Internet, any web addresses or links contained in this book may have changed since publication and may no longer be valid. The views expressed in this work are solely those of the author and do not necessarily reflect the views of the publisher, and the publisher hereby disclaims any responsibility for them.

Dedicated to all the unsung heroes past and present who work in the front line area of law enforcement.

The communities you serve may not thank you enough, but rest assured you are appreciated.

Acknowledgements

My sincere thanks go out to various family members and friends who have helped me in so many ways to bring this book to print.

Some concern has been expressed regarding any real life characters being able to relate to the stories in this book, and therefore I feel it necessary to be non specific in my praise.

My gratitude goes to those who inspired the stories in the first place whether intentional or otherwise, and to the encouragement received from those near to me to complete this book.

Thank you one and all!

Chapter One

"Denby Police emergency, how can I help you?"

"There's a dragon in my living room" said the husky voice of an elderly lady on the other end of the line, "I need help getting it out!"

"Oh no, not another confused nutcase" I thought as I tried to retain my composure and not reflect any disgust in my voice.

"Madam, this is the emergency line, I really don't think we should be dealing with this report on here, could you ring back on local number 626798 and we can take the details from you then?"

It was another busy late Saturday afternoon in mid-summer. I was in the police control room in the relatively sleepy rural market town police station where I was stationed. As an experienced officer I felt confident to deal with most general police duties, but today I had drawn the short straw as I saw it, being given the duty of control room operator in the station rather than being out on the beat.

Pete Knowles, the regular operator, was on annual leave and I guessed that duty sergeant Chris Hobson thought I may appreciate taking the weight off my feet away from street duties. I had done the office duty a few times before and had no worries about being able to handle it, but would have preferred to be out and about doing what I did best.

The set up in the small office which doubled up as a control room cum general office area was such that there was the traditional phone exchange, with three banks of switches to route incoming calls to the various offices and departments, normally operated by a civilian employee, and a single traditional red telephone for incoming emergency calls (in England the 999 system) to be answered by the closest person.

Whenever there were incoming calls on the phone exchange they were indicated by a buzzer and a flashing white light, whereas the red emergency phone rang with the distinctive "ring ring". It could be heard by anyone within the first floor office area, whether they were in the sergeant's office, the crew room, the writing room, parade room or various secretarial and senior officers rooms.

When that phone rang, everyone was aware that a life or death situation may be occurring and that help could be needed instantly by any member of the community, so it was not surprising when people tended to stop what they were doing and listen for that all important call, either shouted down the corridor, or passed out over the radio, to any patrols nearer the scene.

If the all important urgent call was not forthcoming then a sigh of relief went around in the knowledge that whoever had taken the call had deemed it not life threatening, not in their area, or could be dealt with in a different manner, maybe even a hoax call.

"Young man, this is an emergency and I need your help" continued the lady, but this time I detected a little telltale slur in her voice which I had not previously noticed.

Elderly stroke victims may well slur their words, but this would be all the time and cannot be controlled. This sounded like a determined attempt to cover up what was probably an alcohol induced slur, and linking it to the dragon report I couldn't help but put two and two together and decide this was going to be another time waster.

I quickly took the details of the name and address and again asked her to call back on the normal line before quickly ending the call.

Jenny, the civilian operator sitting by the phone exchange in the far corner, glanced over to me as I replaced the receiver, having heard my side of the call and rolled her beautiful green eyes knowingly. She was just about to make a wry comment about people who should know better when the red emergency phone rang again making her jump.

I was right next to it, and as I picked up the receiver and listened as the operator passed the details of the callers' number, I recognised the number as that of the little old lady Mrs Gracie Middleton, the previous caller.

"Police emergency, how can I help you?" I said in my most professional authoritative voice, scarcely daring to know was coming next.

"There is a dragon in my living room" said the familiar voice.

"Mrs Middleton, please could you call back on 626798 and we can take all the details then." I said in as calm a voice as I could muster.

"How do you know my name?" was the bewildered reply.

"Madam, you called me a few minutes ago and I asked you to call on a local line, you must not block the emergency line. This can be dealt with as a non emergency and we can get someone to sort things out if you give us the full details on the other number. Now *please,* hang up and call back on 626798."

I quickly cut off the call before she had chance to utter another word.

"What's all that about?" queried the Chief Inspector Jim Donaldson as he sauntered into the control room from his office having heard the emergency phone ringing twice in quick succession.

"Just some confused drunken grandma with a dragon in her living room" I sighed as I explained the usual method of having dealt with the call.

RING RING—the emergency phone burst into life again.

I had barely had time to move from the spot, so I grabbed the phone angrily and listened quietly as the operator related the caller's number. I was very annoyed and was just about ready to explode down the phone when I realised the number was not the same one as the two previous calls.

"Denby Police emergency, how can I help you?"

"There's been a head on smash on the moors at Liverdale crossroads" said the anxious male caller, "we need an ambulance and rescue gear urgently!!"

I immediately kicked into higher gear, obtaining the necessary details and location whilst passing the details to Jenny to alert ambulance and fire crews by direct line. The switchboard came alive as further calls were coming in from local people reporting the incident, and it quickly became clear that it was a serious accident.

Like a well oiled machine the necessary calls were made, traffic units sent to the scene as co-ordinated details were put into the computer. First officers at the scene requested SOCO (scenes of crime officers) which, although details were not passed over the police radio, (as people listening in on scanners can and do alert the press often with the wrong details) it was readily apparent to me that it was a fatal accident, meaning a lot of resources were going to be tied up for quite a while.

Just then I remembered the calls from the old lady. She lived in a small village some six miles from the accident at Liverdale, but I had already sent the rural area patrol to the scene of the accident and he was going to be tied up for quite a while, so she would have to wait.

In the manic situation it was pointless trying to pass those details over the radio at that time.

RING RING—emergency telephone AGAIN.

I grabbed the phone secretly praying that it was not another serious situation as our already scarce resources were spread very thinly.

As I listened to the caller details I quickly snapped at the operator—"I need to speak to your supervisor NOW."

For the sake of another thirty seconds I was going to keep the line occupied a fraction longer as I quickly relayed the situation to the supervisor and requested a block on emergency calls from the old lady for a four hour period. This is only ever used in extreme cases but I considered that this was just such a case. My reasoning was that after that period she would be asleep and probably not remember the dragon in the morning, and after all, we should have been able to get someone to see her before then.

As Chief Inspector Jim Donaldson had been standing a short distance away it was with respect but frustration that I turned to him with a furrowed brow, with a questioning look in my eyes.

I knew what I had just done was a very serious action which in most cases would have been worthy of checking with a supervisory officer, the typical "cover your arse" syndrome, but felt in the present circumstances I had been justified.

Relief came to me as I watched the wrinkled face of my boss break into his trademark grin, and smiled inwardly as Jim said "what's up Tom, are dragon's not important anymore?"

The lack of a reprimand and the joke made me feel at ease, as did the knowledge that I didn't have to go explain the situation in his office.

Just then a call came in over the force wide radio requesting supervision at the scene of the traffic accident, a sure sign that things were not getting any better. Saturday afternoon is not a good time at best, and as Jim shot a glance at the clock, he turned on his heel to go get his reflective jacket, shouting to Jenny to call his wife at home (a much too frequent occurrence) and tell her he would be late coming home and to explain the situation.

As time went on and the accident scene became stabilised, the usual evening time calls came in, rowdy youths, domestic disputes and the rest, I was kept busy.

It turned out to be a long evening shift and before I knew it the first of the nightshift were turning up.

I was preparing the computer files for closure by the duty sergeant, pleased that the numbers were reducing, I suddenly became aware of a single line entry—"dragon."

"Oh my god!" I thought to myself, "not only has it not been dealt with, it was an incoming 999 call and I had requested that it would be blocked".

I had become so engrossed in everything else that this incident had just completely slipped my mind. I had always tried to be an efficient and fair officer and was proud of the fact that, to date, I had managed to avoid any complaints, the scourge of any serving officer. Now I could see the full force of the rubber heel squad (police internal complaints division) bearing down on me.

As the nightshift officer replacement walked in through the front door, I could see the returning figure of our Chief Inspector on the security cameras coming in the rear doors.

Oh Boy, I would have to act fast.

"Back in a minute" I shouted to my night shift relief as I dashed out of the door. I intercepted the weary figure of my boss in the rear stairwell, and breathlessly confessed my oversight, offering to go out immediately myself to try to sort out this mess. To avoid any conflicts with the nightshift manning I asked if I could use the supervision car, which after all was mainly parked up in the back yard. Jim had certainly seen and heard many things in his career, and was acutely aware at how damaging a complaint against the station could be, particularly a 999 call of which he was aware.

"OK Tom, do what you can, I'll stop on until you get back, make sure you . . . ."

He stopped mid sentence as we both heard the distant familiar ringing of the 999 emergency telephone from up in the control room. "Just sort it out as best you can."

I made my way back to the control room but as I did so I encountered a familiar yet haggard figure coming towards me. It was Joe D'Arcy, the rural beat bobby for the area around Liverdale.

He had been assigned the unfortunate job of dealing with the two fatal casualties and had just returned from the hospital after having dealt with the relatives of the deceased and the necessary paperwork.

"Not only does it rain, but it pours" I thought.

"Joe, I know you have had one hell of a shift, can you tell me if you know of a Gracie Middleton at Honeysuckle cottage in . . . ?"

"What about her?" snapped Joe.

"Well, it's like this" I said as I filled Joe in with the details.

"Oh hell" said Joe "she is very well placed with the WI, and I don't care how much she likes a drop of the hard stuff, she needs dealing with delicately."

"Look, it's my mess" I said, "I've got the bosses' car keys and I'll go over."

"OK, but I'm nearly finished here so will join you if you like, it's on my way home."

"Cheers mate" I said as Joe dashed off.

As I arrived in the control room I was greeted by a very puzzled nightshift operator.

"There is an entry about Dragon on the computer, but Jenny told me not to do anything with it just yet. I've just had a 999 call from the operations supervisor to say the call block has been taken off . . . . What's it all about?"

"Don't even ASK?!" I said.

I quickly said I was going to sort it out, it was under the radar and not for anyone else to hear about, otherwise not only me but the boss was going to be in the proverbial. I quickly handed over the other incident details, quietly drew a radio and sneaked out of the back door to the waiting supervision car.

As I drove as quickly but restrained as I could to the beautiful rural moors area, my head was swimming with the possible full implications if she made a fuss. It was only as I got nearer that I realised that the address was only a house name, it was going to be difficult to locate. This is where the detailed knowledge of the local bobby becomes invaluable.

The last thing I wanted to have to do was go into the local pub, the only place open at this time on a Saturday night. Tentatively I picked up the car radio transmitter handset, calling the call sign of my colleague Joe D'Arcy's rural beat car.

To my great relief the crackly signal came back. Without giving too much away I arranged a rendezvous at the local village green and within ten minutes Joe's car came into view. As he drove past, Joe gave the signal to follow him and within half a mile the two marked police cars pulled up at the entrance to a long gravel driveway leading to a quaint ivy covered cottage set well back from the road.

"Let's get this over with" I thought to myself as Joe climbed out of his car. The evening twilight was closing in, and the lack of street lighting made it somewhat eerie. I took the big torch from the back of the car and used it to illuminate the drive, but just as we approached the house the area was bathed in light as the security lights came on.

This obviously alerted the occupant of the house as I saw a figure appear at the side window peering out through the lace curtain, her frail figure illuminated by the wall light behind her.

Before we had chance to knock, the door swung open and the tiny white haired figure of Gracie Middleton stood in the centre of the doorway. As she steadied herself on her one walking stick, I desperately racked my brains for a suitable opening gambit.

She recognised Joe and a slight smile flashed across her withered features, then she shot a glance towards me.

"Have you finished with the accident then?" she asked wearily, "I heard it was bad so thought you might be late."

"Wow, there is a God" I thought, but before I had chance to say anything Joe interrupted me.

"Yes Gracie, it was bad. Young kid from the next village and a tourist." His tone of voice was one not to be messed with.

"I fell asleep waiting" Gracie said, "but it is still there, it's gone to sleep under the sideboard."

I took this chance to interject, "Maybe now will be a good time to catch it."

"I don't want it catching, I want it chasing away" said Gracie in a startling clear and shrill voice.

She turned to shuffle back into the open plan kitchen, and as I entered I caught sight of the empty whisky bottle on the farmhouse style dresser along the back wall.

Joe caught my eye and we both shared a knowing grin. Drink and time do not mix, the old lady would probably not remember when she first called, and the long time difference may not register, coupled with the fact that she had been asleep, there may be light at the end of the complaint tunnel.

She was remarkably steady as she shuffled along, so I assumed she may not be too much under the influence, I had no way of knowing how much had been in the bottle when she started drinking.

"What does it look like?" Joe asked innocently.

"It looks like a dragon of course" shrilled Gracie, "what do you expect?"

"No, no, I meant what colour is it?" stammered Joe.

"It's green and long" commented Gracie.

"That's good" I said, leaping to Joe's rescue, "the pink ones can be very nasty!"

The look from Joe was pure scorn, trying not to laugh out loud.

"Look Gracie, we need a plan." said Joe. "How do you think it got in?"

"I went to put the washing out, and when I came back in, there it was, snorting fire by the hearth," exclaimed Gracie.

"Aha, a back draft down the chimney as the door was opened was the probable cause" I thought to myself.

"Right then, so all we need to do is chase it out. But, you realise we will have to run after it and close the door quickly behind us. If we come back in it might get past us, so once we are out, we will leave, is that OK?" I said aloud.

"That sounds good" Gracie mumbled.

"And once we are gone we can chase it out of the village. Is there anything else you want us to do? Anything else may be bothering you? We just like to know everything was dealt with as you wanted."

"That will be fine, but I wasn't happy with the officer I talked to on the phone, he was very abrupt."

"She doesn't recognise my voice" I thought, and then out loud I said;

"OK, I will have a word with our Chief Inspector and tell him the details" I said in all honesty.

"So, what we need to do is open both doors and then we will be able to chase it out. The problem is Joe and I can't see it, because they make themselves invisible to police officers when inside buildings, so you need to tell us where it is and tell us when it runs out of the door, OK? We will be able to see it outside though. You just close the doors after we chase it out"

"Right then, under the sideboard you say" Joe stated matter-of-factly.

He pulled his truncheon out of the special pocket down the side of his uniform trousers, as I quickly caught on, pulling my own truncheon out. We both stood there brandishing our truncheons in an aggressive manner to deal with the evil dragon slumbering under the sideboard.

I opened the outside door of the kitchen and asked Gracie to stand behind it and get ready to slam it shut behind us as we pursued the offending green dragon snorting smoke and fire out of her home.

I opened the living room door and could see the sideboard was in full view of the door, and Gracie could see it from where she was standing.

"Make this look good Joe!" I muttered just loud enough for him to hear. Joe dropped to his knees, whilst then on all fours; he started to make prodding gestures under the sideboard in a markedly determined effort to wake up the monster.

Just then the big grandfather clock struck the half hour making us both jump. But that was it!! The dragon apparently woke up as Gracie shouted out "it's moving!"

With a wild thrashing motion both of us lunged under the sideboard with our truncheon, shouting and making as much noise as possible.

"It's coming out" shouted Gracie.

We both moved together across the room towards the door, and to our relief heard Gracie shout "it's running across the kitchen, quick close the door."

We raced across the kitchen and shouted over our shoulders "goodnight Gracie", as we slammed the door behind us and continued running up the driveway to the cars.

As we got round the corner out of sight from the house we both burst out laughing. After the sort of day we had both had, this unexpected piece of light relief had come at the right time.

I realised that I was way over my allocated shift, and no way dare I claim overtime for this escapade, and of course Joe was late as well. I said my heartfelt thanks to Joe, bid him goodnight as he disappeared into the now darkened village street towards his car.

As I prepared to set off I realised it would take time to get back to the station, I called Denby on the force radio. To my surprise Jim Donaldson came on the air, he had obviously been waiting anxiously for the outcome before he returned home many hours late. I proudly announced "incident dealt with, all resolved, no complaints!!"

The relief in Jim's voice was evident as he seriously asked (bearing in mind force control were monitoring this transmission) "and what about the intruder?"

"Last seen running across the moors, no damage caused and nothing missing! The complainant was satisfied with action taken. Over and out." I said with a grin as I replaced the handset.

"Hee hee" I thought laughing inwardly, "the things we have to do."

But then it hit me! Who had had the last laugh??

A lonely old lady had just seen two burly police officers on hands and knees, brandishing truncheons, chasing an invisible green dragon out of her house late at night. What better entertainment on a Saturday night could she get at the tax payers expense?

Maybe she wasn't as daft as she seemed.

Chapter Two

"These are a few of the do's and don'ts" were the well meaning words of advice from the time served police van driver Mick Willis.

I had just arrived in the small fishing town of Denby on the North West coast of England. It was quite a come down from the large inner city force I had just left, and I could see that a few adjustments would have to be made.

Life in the big city had become mundane and predictable. The area I had lived in with my wife Angela and our three children had become run down and somewhat miserable, and it was with eyes wide open that I had requested a transfer to the small rural town.

I had joined the Police Force with an overriding desire to help people. The big town policing was impersonal and devoid of meaningful contact with the public. I was just a faceless figure in a uniform.

It was important to me as a family man to feel I was making a positive difference to people's lives.

"We don't have the manpower to handle big situations, so you tread carefully" Mick continued, "and always keep an ear on the radio so you know what everyone else is doing. Don't expect back up if a couple of cars are at the other side of town." He said with an air of apprehension.

"The locals will fight amongst themselves, but will all stick together if an outside group come in. You'll soon get to know the local characters."

It was my first nightshift out in the town, I was cruising the town centre as a passenger in the general purpose police van. Whereas in my previous town there would be up to eight officers in the van ready to hit trouble instantly, there was just the two of us.

The drinking laws were still the same as post war, everywhere closed at eleven with twenty minutes drinking up time. When would the powers that be realise this produced the biggest flash point of the night, all the brawlers out on the street at the same time?

As the minutes ticked by I became increasingly aware of the size of the town. It took us just fifteen minutes to do a slow circuit covering most of the pubs. One thing that struck me immediately was that this was up close and personal. I could see myself dealing with the same people time and again, something I looked forward to in a weird sort of way.

Our beat was general cover for the town area. There were a few foot patrols in town, then a couple of area car drivers for the outskirts, with traffic patrols and rural officers further out in the surrounding moors area. A typical weekend night would give rise to more patrols being closer to the town centre for obvious reasons.

There was only ever one chance to make a first impression, and I realised that I needed to make a good one. I refused to be intimidated by the yobs walking the streets, shouting obscenities at the van every time it went past.

One in particular was a large muscular youth covered in tattoos with a shaven head. He didn't quite go as far as the bovver boots of the earlier skinheads, but would not have been out of place.

"Who is the mouth on legs?" I asked as the youth yelled once again as the van went past.

"That's Johnny "Nutter" Lawson" said Mick, driving slowly past, "a real bad piece of work just came out two weeks ago after a stretch for GBH."

I could tell from his voice that he was scared of him.

The van parked up for a while at the central crossroads. After a short while a couple of the foot beat officers stopped by for a chat, at the same time as Nutter Johnny was moving between pubs, still shouting obscenities.

"Why do we put up with that sort of behaviour?" I said out loud.

"'Cos they are all the same. He has no fear when he's popped up," said Bob Turley, a stocky family man in his mid forties who had been in the town many years.

"It's not fear they need, it's respect" I said, causing an unintended round of laughter from the rest.

"They wouldn't know respect if it bit them on the arse" laughed Bob.

"It is always the same old thing. Out for a few pints, push their luck and see if they get locked up, sleep it off and out in the morning" said Robin Needham standing next to Bob.

"Why don't the magistrates sort them out?" I asked creating yet another round of giggles.

"The yobs know where they live, so any attempt at sorting them out results in hassle" said Bob.

"Oh for god's sake, the nutters are running the asylum!" I said. "Isn't it about time we stood up to them?"

"We just collect the bruises for our troubles" moaned Robin.

"Has nobody heard of the ways and means act anymore?" I asked, frustrated at their attitude. "There is more than one way to skin a cat you know!"

"What do you have in mind?" asked Bob intrigued.

"Well, I'm the new boy on the block so nobody knows me. If we get a run in with them tonight, they will expect to be locked up, sleep it off and be out in the morning, right?"

"I bet they are so out of it they can't remember much either? Then here's my plan."

I went on to explain what they could do, with me ready to take the blame if it went pear shaped. You could see the others were tempted, about time they had a chance to turn the tables.

"What about Sarge" asked Bob, "he won't like It." said the van driver Mick.

"What is there to tell him? If it goes right he will be too busy to be any the wiser and he will get a quieter night." I said.

"Disturbance at the Kings Head" came the radio report. Bob and Robin were off through one of the back alleys as a shortcut to the pub just as Mick started up the van and raced around the one way system.

When we arrived there was a large group of people outside, a lot of shouting, pushing and pulling. It looked like the womenfolk had sorted out their men and whatever disagreement there had been appeared to have been sorted out. Nobody came forward with any complaints so it was easier to keep a background presence.

It was that time of night when the resentment would simmer for a while, and unless the combatants went in opposite directions then it would erupt again. There was always an aggressor who had a point to prove, and a target that was not going to be pushed around but didn't really want to fight.

When their mates held them back they were mouthy and showy but didn't have the heart for a scrap. That is until several drinks later, stares across crowded bars and boom, off they go again.

I was always amazed when it came to pub fights.

Those in the know knew who the hard men were.

The hard men knew who they were.

They didn't need to start trouble, but would always end it.

Then there came the noisy yobs. They too knew who the hard men were and conveniently stayed out of their pubs.

The yobs who fancied themselves tended to move in groups like pack animals, they never had the guts to go it alone. If they didn't have their mates around them, no audience to play to and no back up if they bit off more than they could chew, they were nobody.

Gutless bullies not long out of the school yard. You only ever had to be on a prison escort to realise the difference. Take them from their band of mates, put them through those big gates and watch them jump.

Those who knew the system, and those who didn't soon did, made sure they did what was necessary to play the game. If the screws didn't get them the arse bandits would, who were the hard men now?

So as not to inflame the situation Mick pulled the van a short distance away and the foot patrols looked on from the other side of the street. There was still about twenty minutes to the big kick out.

One group from outside the Kings headed quickly back to the crossroads, they would do the last minute dash to get served. The eleven o'clock deadline nearly always got stretched this way, and the locals knew which landlords would oblige and which ones wouldn't.

From what we could make out the troublemaker from the previous incident had been with the group which had left.

It would only be a matter of time before something else kicked off nearby.

Almost immediately the radio sparked into life, a fight outside the "Shoulder of Mutton" pub. Now I knew I would be faster jumping out of the van and running up the link alleyway, as the van would need to go all the way round the one way system. I leapt out, conscious of the fact that the two foot patrol officers Bob and Robin had started walking quickly in that direction, as I broke into a full paced run.

Because I was running I obviously got to the scene first, as I ran round the corner I was just in time to see "Nutter Lawson" swinging several punches at another person nearly half his size.

Without even hesitating I ran between them and grabbed the very surprised "Nutter" in a vice like arm lock. I could see the astonishment on his face as he had turned to see who had the balls to take him on. He started screaming obscenities and struggled to get out of the arm lock.

I knew from bitter experience that unless someone came to my aid soon I would lose my grip. I quickly kicked the Nutter on the back of his right leg, causing him to buckle and fall to the floor, a far better position to hold him down.

As I pinned him face down to the ground I felt a weight on my back as one of the Nutters "gang" tried getting me off, then more weight as others piled in.

I had earned the nickname "The Terrier" when I was fresh out of training, once I got hold of a prisoner I was not one to let go, and I had no intentions of starting now!

I held on tight as the muffled screams and bellows of "Nutter Lawson" came from beneath me. As quickly as it happened the weight came off as I realised the cavalry had arrived and I heard the van screech to a halt.

The commotion continued on around me as I realised others were being arrested and put into the van. My quarry wriggled and cursed below me but I held tight.

It seemed to go quiet as I managed to glance round. The back doors of the van were being held shut by a guy I now know to be the landlord of the Shoulder of Mutton, as the other officers came to my aid. Knowing if Nutter was put with his mates he would be even more of a handful, I yelled to get another car. As it happened one of the rural officers, Joe D'Arcy, who happened to be in town had responded to the call and had just arrived on the scene.

It was, unfortunately, one of the Ford Fiesta run around cars! As I heard the others say the van was leaving it left me and the rural bobby to deal with "Nutter." Having got his hands cuffed behind his back it was going to be nigh on impossible to get him into the car.

After several unsuccessful attempts I decided the ways and means act was called for. I told Joe, to open both back doors. I then propelled "Nutter" head first towards the back seat. As soon as his head and shoulders were in, I motioned to Joe push.

I ran round the other side, grabbed hold of "the Nutter" by both of his ears and pulled.

With a shrill scream he lunged forward across the back seat before I pushed his head down behind the drivers' seat.

With his hands behind his back there was not a lot his Lordship could do except kick out with his feet.

I wound down the back nearside passenger window so he couldn't kick the glass out, then closed the door carefully, allowing the gangly legs of "the Nutter" to protrude out of the window space. The more he tried to kick, the more his shins got damaged!

Much to my surprise, a cheer went up from the small group watching the melee as I jumped into the passenger seat and reached over to restrain his legs.

As Joe got in the car I grinned a mischievous smile. He told me he was just about to finish his shift and go home.

"Well, well" I thought, "How convenient!"

Now, Joe didn't know the plan which had been hatched earlier. I had got the others to agree that, instead of taking any rowdy "prisoners" to the police station, they would drive them out of town some ten miles and kick them out on the surrounding desolate moors.

The reasoning went like this. The yobs were normally that drunk they didn't know what they were doing and could not remember anything the next morning. There were no phone boxes up on the moors to call for a taxi even if they knew where they were (long before the concept of mobile phones.) By the time they found their way home all fight would be out of them, they wouldn't recognise who had done the dirty deed, less work for the custody sergeant and no paperwork.

As it happens the rural beat bobby would not be out of place going home, and a traffic car could pick me up on the way back.

A brief non committal chat on the radio with the van driver confirmed the van load had indeed been taken to the station, so the sergeant would be busy. Joe called the traffic car and arranged a meet up on the moors, a commonplace occurrence so nothing untoward in the radio transmission.

With that we headed out of town, muffled yells from the back of the driver seat and a chilly breeze with the back window open.

As we reached the rendezvous point the traffic car was already there. In the darkness the now dazed and utterly confused "Nutter" was unceremoniously hauled out from the patrol car.

You could see the cogs slowly turning in his Neanderthal brain. No street lights, no people, just four police officers in the darkness. He was told to walk in the downhill direction and stick to the road! Handcuffs off, four uniformed officers watching him and no crowd to play to, the hapless bully accepted his lot and tottered off like a good little boy.

I waved a farewell to Joe who continued to his home beat, as the traffic car sped back into town to cover my absence. Just in time for a scheduled break, I walked in with a big grin as the others looked quizzically and mouthed "where is he?" without actually saying anything. "Mine got away" I lied. The ways and means act strikes again!!

The word was passed quietly around for mobile patrols to watch out for Nutter walking his way into town. It was just after four in the morning that I glimpsed the sorry figure of Johnny Lawson walking forlornly along the High Street towards his home. Although the police van was the only vehicle moving, it was easy to spot, as we drove past there was no sound of any taunting abusive obscenities directed towards the van.

It came to my knowledge later that duty sergeant Chris Hobson had commented that the new guy apparently hadn't got involved in the incident or made an arrest, not a very good start! The rest of the guys knew I had taken far longer reaching action.

Several days later I was just finishing a late evening foot patrol, making my way along the riverside frontage when I saw Johnny and a couple of his mates coming towards me. One of the lads made a grunting sound as I approached, something I was well used to and was like water off a ducks back. I never reacted to those taunts. As he did so, Johnny thumped him quickly to shut him up and I heard him say "Don't fuck with that one Don."

He obviously remembered something of the fuzzy Saturday night then.

It was music to my ears as I walked past the little group, a wry smile and a wink to Johnny as I went past. An excellent first impression I think!!

Chapter Three

Trying to settle in to the new small town way of doing things, I was finding every day a steep learning curve. Of course one of the biggest challenges was finding my way around.

Who do people ask if they want to know where something is or how to get somewhere? Ask a policeman!

If the policeman doesn't know it doesn't exactly inspire confidence. Also, whenever an incident happens, it is always good to know the fastest way there and/or a place to intercept if a chase is ongoing.

To my surprise as the briefing before the night duty was coming to an end, I found out that I was being allocated an area car beat to the south of the little town. With no hard and fast rules, basically if anything occurred south of an imaginary line drawn west–east across the town map and it was better to send a car than a foot patrol; I would get first call if I was available.

A second surprise was that I was being doubled up with a young fiery WPC688 Kath Montgomery. Although pretty small in stature, what she lacked in height was made up from a real go getter no nonsense attitude.

Kath had been in the town some seven months so in theory knew the street layout a lot better than me. For me to be the allocated driver that made Kath the extra body available as initial response, and she could well end up dealing with the incident if I was required elsewhere.

As we made our way out into the late night traffic, I quickly settled into the smaller patrol car than I had been used to in my other force. Kath was easy to talk to but just a little bit too inquisitive about personal matters. I quickly realised that she was a potential gossip and I would have to watch exactly what I gave away in idle conversation.

Likewise, as soon as I asked reciprocal questions, she was a little bit too liberal with the answers, wearing her heart on her sleeve prepared to discuss matters which quite frankly I felt I would rather not know!

I had spent many hours with a town map, learning and relearning first the major roads and then the side roads. What I did find infuriating was that many places or landmarks would have a local name, the origins of which had long since disappeared.

For instance, if someone reported a crash at Colliers crossroads, you had to know the local history as the scrap merchant John Collier, who once owned large premises at the crossroads and had died long ago, the site was now a sparkling car sales room.

It was also a good idea to learn the names and locations of all the public houses. First of all because they were brilliant landmarks and relatively easy to find and identify, but secondly because there was more than a remote chance that trouble would originate either in or near to them.

As I familiarised myself with the area with the aid of Kath, we dealt with a couple of minor calls. There had been one domestic and one alarm activation.

There was something else which was not written on the town map. I soon realised the local names of the various estates had to be learned quickly. The name was often associated with the clustered street names so it was relatively easy to remember, yet others were just local labels without any apparent origin.

It was a quiet night, not a lot of calls and nothing much happening on the streets. Just as we were considering making our way in for a meal break we received a call to attend a disturbance at the nearby Marquis Hotel.

I already knew the location as it was near to where my kids had started school, and I impressed Kath by my knowledge of a shortcut which cut out two sets of traffic lights and got us there a lot faster.

A group of people were outside on the pavement. As we got out of the marked police car the usual grunts and calls were made which never phased me anymore. We made our way into the "hotel."

The place was a rundown drinking joint which had probably not had paying resident guests in years. As we entered there was intense activity by a small band of musicians frantically packing their equipment away and trying to get it out to their waiting van.

"It's that group of four outside that started it!" shouted one hysterical girl hardly old enough to be out of school, let alone out at night, mascara smudged around her tear stained eyes making her look like a panda.

We were then approached by a guy who turned out to be the bar manager who led us back towards the entrance.

"Those four have had far too much to drink" he said. "I tried to kick them out but they got stroppy and had a go at me and the lads."

"Is anyone hurt?" Kath asked, looking round for any likely injuries.

"I don't think so, just a bit shocked that's all" said the manager.

"Are there any complaints or allegations that you need us to follow up" she clarified.

"No, but I'd like them clearing from the front door if possible" he said with a sigh of relief.

"Easier said than done" I thought. Public places and reluctant drunks are time consuming, they knew even if they moved on a little bit it was difficult to deal with them.

We emerged outside into the cold air, amazed that anyone would want to hang around.

Then again, somebody with a skin full of alcohol never seemed to feel the cold. We identified the four in question, not very difficult as they were the ones making the grunting noises!

I decided up close and personal was the way I was going to play it. I approached the group and as always chose the biggest. For some reason I thought I recognised the guy but just couldn't place him.

He was a good six feet three inches tall, heavily built with long straight greasy black hair in a central parting keeping his eyes in shadow, wearing denim jacket and jeans with distinctive tan coloured cowboy boots. As I approached he spat defiantly onto the floor, just missing my immaculately polished boot.

"So, just what appears to be the problem gents?" I asked politely yet firmly. They all seemed to speak at once! From what I could establish they were members of a pop group which had previously been booked to play the venue. It turned out they had been dropped in favour of the other obviously outgoing band. They had turned up to see the competition and a bit of rivalry had erupted.

"OK, so you've had your dig, let's call it quits and go home please" pleaded Kath.

The four were obviously very much the worse for wear through too much booze. They mumbled something or other about police harassment but moved along a little.

When Kath and I reached the car, I asked,

"Did you recognise any of them, particularly the big one?"

"No, I don't think so" Kath said in a considered tone.

"Funny, I don't know why but there was something about him" I replied. If Kath had no recollections it was not likely to have been a matter at briefing or the bulletin board.

We were just about half way back to the nick having called in to report all quiet when we received an urgent radio call "Fire brigade attending the Marquis!"

Because we were already out on the streets and close by, we would reach the Marquis before the fire tenders. I deftly swung the car round and raced off back from whence we came.

As we neared the hotel something wasn't right. There were no crowds out on the pavement, no sign of smoke, no alarm bells or anything untoward.

We screeched to a halt and ran into the entrance to the amusement of several drunken people. The bar manager just happened to be nearby collecting glasses and caught our eye.

"There has been a fire call put through, what's the problem?" I said.

"I don't think so" said the manager glancing at the fire panel on the back wall.

The sound of two tone alarms and the hissing of air brakes announced the arrival of the first fire engine, shortly followed by another and a turntable ladder unit. The entrance hall was transformed into what appeared to be a blue light disco as the lights of their warning beacons bounced off the various surfaces.

A quick check of the fire alarm panel, and I went to intercept the lead fire fighter to warn him of a hoax call. As usual all the necessary checks had to be made, but as a precaution they cleared out the remaining revellers effectively closing the place for the night.

I radioed control to let them know, but also asked them to check the origin of the call. I reckoned the telephone number would tie up with the call box outside the nearby post office. When I went to look I could see the receiver dangling off the hook still swinging. No surprises there!

It did not take Sherlock Holmes to make an educated guess at just who may have been responsible for the call. The four band members previously ejected were sitting on a wall some fifty yards away, but I had no proof.

The fire engines departed quickly to be back at their base in readiness for a genuine call. Several neighbours were to be seen peering out of curtained windows wondering what all the commotion had been about.

Everything quietened down as Kath and I sat outside the hotel in the car making up our pocket books.

"Time for a cuppa" Kath said jubilantly.

"Erm, I don't think so." I said in a discouraging way. "I don't think we've finished here yet. Something tells me they will try it again. Firstly to annoy us, secondly to annoy the hotel, and finally for some perverted sense of fun in seeing the engines turn out."

"Let me have a look at the street map" I said, "I have a plan"

I quickly found our location, and then had a look at the back street layout.

I wanted to be seen to drive off towards the town centre as before, but then double back and try to come out nearly opposite the phone box, or at least in a place from where it could be observed. I showed Kath the route chosen, then drove off as normal. I also asked Kath to contact control and let us know instantly when any emergency 999 call came in while the caller was on the line.

We quickly found our way round the back streets, but as I turned into the chosen street and turned the vehicle lights off, slowly making my way to the top end, the radio sparked into life.

"688—Incoming 999"

I immediately put my lights back on and floored it to get to the top of the street. As we got there the phone box door was just closing, with the receiver swinging freely. I caught sight of the tall band member running down the next side street.

Of all the times it could happen, an oncoming car on the main road delayed my emergence. As I got to the side street there was no sign of the guy.

Just then we heard a car starting up, and both saw a dark shape moving away from a parking space at the bottom of the street, without lights. In a flash we were back in the car, blue lights on racing in the direction of the departing car.

"My God" I exclaimed, "he could hardly stand up let alone drive!"

The other band members were nowhere to be seen. Kath contacted control and confirmed the chase was on and to cancel the fire brigade if that call had been from the same number. They confirmed it had.

We quickly got close to the fleeing car. The roads were narrowed on both sides with parked cars such that there was only room for one car even though we were in fact two way streets. There was no way of passing him, just following; fortunately very little other traffic was around at that time of night.

As Kath tried her best to keep up a commentary, the ever changing back streets just became a blur as we raced in and out, up and down. Given the fact the guy appeared drunk I was surprised the way he could handle his car, even without his lights on.

He hurtled across the main road and back into a maze of side streets, I momentarily lost sight of him but a quick flash of brake lights gave his location away at the bottom of the street.

As we got there we could see the man get out and run across the road. I mustn't let him get into the house as I was not sure of any power of entry, as I couldn't be one hundred per cent sure that this was the drunken band member, but it sure looked like him.

I chased him up the short garden path; I saw the tan cowboy boots and was now certain it was him. As the guy fumbled with his keys I grabbed him from behind telling him he was under arrest on suspicion of drunk driving.

Unfortunately the man had managed to get his door open. I tripped him as he stepped into the door entrance, the door flung open and a very excitable small dog, later to be seen as a Jack Russell, started yelping and making dashes towards us.

As all hell had let loose I shouted to Kath to get some help. Problem was she didn't know exactly where we were after the chase! The landing light came on as a dishevelled figure of a sleepy woman in a dressing gown appeared at the top of the stairs.

"What the hell is going on" she shrieked, seeing a police officer wrestling with her husband in the confines of the entrance door. I was still on top and managed to shout at her,

"What's this address?" in an urgent and desperate manner.

"22 Godwin Street, why do you want to know?" She shrieked back.

I glanced over my shoulder and saw that Kath had heard that and was on the radio for some back up. It was all fine and well having a female colleague, but there was no way she could be expected to wrestle with this big guy without getting hurt.

Kath literally climbed over us to fend off the yapping dog and shouted at the woman to get it under control. The cries of a child could be heard upstairs as the commotion had woken the household, and no doubt a few others.

The man was swearing and cursing underneath me. Although I knew I could not move him myself, I held him firmly on the floor. The woman could be heard ranting at the dog, the kids and the officers all at once.

At last the flashing lights of another emergency vehicle filled the street, and soon I had another couple of male colleagues to help me extricate the drunken driver. We got him cuffed and into the waiting police van, made sure we had his car keys and left a very confused wife and mother at the house.

As we compared notes and filled in our pocket books we made sure that our accounts of the incident matched and that all evidential procedures were correct. I was annoyed with myself at not being totally sure of the correct way of dealing with a hoax 999 caller but was sure it was only a reportable offence. The drink driving meanwhile was not going to be a problem.

The drunken driver reeked of alcohol as we booked him into the custody area. He gave his details freely which matched up with the address he had run into, and stood sheepishly as he went through the breath testing procedure.

As expected, the test revealed he was more than three times over the drink driving limit. Something still niggled at me as I made a few background checks on the guy without any significant result.

In the case of a drink driver, local policy was to charge them and let them sober up in the cells. Provided they did not have access to another car or set of keys, they were often released about half an hour before the early turn shift arrived at six a.m, thus leaving the cells clear and less of a job to hand over.

As he was charged I included in the list of dirty deeds dangerous driving, (as in no lights) driving whilst over the prescribed limit, wasting police time, hoax calls and a couple of minor paperwork technicalities. He was then placed in a cell to sober up.

Kath and I now got chance to have that long awaited cuppa. As was usually the case, we had it whilst making our witness statements to the events of the evening, as heaven knows when the next chance might be. If anything unusual arose the following day, it was far better to have a statement prepared in our tray where daytime supervision could find it, rather than getting an unwanted wake up call.

At quarter past five I made my way to the cell area to wake the sleeping beauty and kick him out. He had been sleeping for three hours so I was sure he would not be fit to drive, but all the same I would give him a quick breath test to check.

It was always an unpleasant experience dealing with the morning after the night before drunk. Their breath invariably stank. When I first started the job I resolved to carry a packet of mints with me to offer to the prisoner, but later found that the sweets may interfere with the breath test so I couldn't use them and had to suffer their halitosis.

This guy turned out to be no exception to the experience; I kept as much distance between us as I could. I quickly prepared the hand held alcometer and got him to provide a sample.

Ping!

The indicator immediately jumped straight to red!

"Strange" I thought, it generally takes a while longer.

"What were you drinking last night?" I asked.

"A few ciders" came the croaky response.

"Crikey, I think they're still fermenting inside you!" I remarked.

This created a bit of a dilemma. It wasn't usual to do a second screening test but the custody officer just didn't have time. The case had been proven, and another test would establish if his reading had increased as more alcohol had been absorbed into his bloodstream. We needed him out of the cells.

"Do you have another set of car keys?" I asked.

"No, don't think so," was the reply.

"Right, I'm going to let you go, but be warned you will not be safe to drive until after lunch at the earliest. You'll be able to pick up your keys at the front desk after that."

With a grunt and a forced grin he was shown out of the secure area.

A quick final check, vehicle logbook filled in and I was good to head home. It had been another busy shift and not too much of a paperwork headache.

As I arrived home I was surprised to see Angela and middle child up and about. Both were still in pyjamas, it turned out he had been up nearly all night with sickness and diarrhoea, numerous bed and pyjama changes later. They both looked shattered.

It was surprising how one could adapt to doing night shifts. For someone not used to being up through the night it comes as a tremendous shock to the system. Fortunately Angela was not due in to her volunteering job until lunchtime. Finding a reserve of strength from somewhere I got the other two kids washed and dressed for school, as Mum and patient went back to bed.

I was in the process of dropping the kids off at school when I glanced across at the school gates.

"Kerching!" the penny dropped. I saw my prisoner from the previous night waving bye to a little lad running into the playground. That was it; he was, after all, just another parent doing the school run.

"I wonder what his missus had had to say when he got home!" I mused as I made my own way home.

Chapter Four

Friday afternoon two 'clock came around and I was actually finished on time. The off going shift members were in high spirits as it was the end of the shift pattern and we could look forward to three days off duty.

There would be plenty of time to spend with Angela and kids, get caught up on some chores and gardening, and have a little fun, and maybe some decent sleep!

That night was to be one of the younger lads on the shift's 21st birthday celebration, and as per usual everyone on the shift was invited. As everyone was off duty together it was natural that they got together when they could for relevant celebrations. The blanket invitation always went out, but it was well known that various members would not attend for a multitude of reasons, but tonight was going to be a sit down meal at a local curry house, then on to a nightclub.

Jeff, the birthday boy, needed to know who was intending to go, whether partners were included or not so that he could book the tables. A grand total of twenty one people were joining him to celebrate his birthday. They were not all police officers, as well as the spouses and partners there were also a few clerical and civilian staff.

The doorbell at home rang on the dot of seven o'clock as our babysitter Helen arrived, leaving myself and Angela plenty of time to walk slowly down to the town centre pub where the original meeting would take place. As it was still early the kids were not yet in bed, but they enjoyed being looked after by Helen who had plenty of teenage energy and ideas to keep them amused.

We also suspected that they got a bit of a treat by staying up a little bit later than we would have allowed, but it was the weekend ahead after all and I was sure we would welcome a bit of a lie in as well. We said our goodnights, scarcely noticed as the kids were already involved in some sort of hide and seek game as Helen had hidden a small packet of sweets somewhere and of course they were all intent on being the lucky finder.

It was a pleasant night so we walked slowly, not giving a thought to later weather conditions as we expected to just jump into a waiting taxi outside the club and get dropped off at home.

Presents had been given earlier to Jeff, so that would save him having to carry them or leave them somewhere overnight.

As it happened when we were half way to the first pub the sky turned dark and we quickened our pace in the anticipation that a shower was on its way, we arrived just in time as the first few spots of rain began to fall. As we were settling in to the second round, some latecomers arrived huffing and puffing, and also very wet.

"Damn!" I thought as I realised we had not brought raincoats or an umbrella. Hopefully it would only be a shower so moving around the town would not be a problem.

The pub had been chosen as it was next door but one to the curry house, so when the time came to round everyone up and move across there was no big drama and no ruined hairstyles in the process. Many of the spouses and partners knew each other as there had been several successful social nights with the shift, and several of the kids attended the same schools, so they had the usual school gate chatter to catch up on.

There was no particular seating plan so people just drifted together with their preferred friends. The members of staff in the restaurant were very efficient and soon the starters were being dished out.

Now as happens in all walks of life, but in the police especially, there are some people who just do not recognise that people who do a particular job do, in fact, have a life outside that job. As would be obvious, the off duty officers would, at some time or other, be recognised by the people they deal with on a regular basis. What is also apparent is that many of these people have been locked up for their actions. They tend to wear it as a badge of honour, and any chance encounter with off duty officers can and does lead to conflict.

Across the small restaurant was another family gathering, but this time it was of a well known loud mouthed villain whose dislike of the force was well documented and he took every chance to let everyone know about it.

It could be anticipated that when police officers went out socially there was always going to be a risk of being verbally insulted, which is why the majority preferred to travel out of town for a night out. Tonight was different because of the numbers.

Normally the more experienced officers would just let any comment go unanswered so as not to provoke any reaction, but unfortunately tonight some of the younger officers had started drinking early, and by now their high spirits were also accompanied by lower tolerance thresholds to unwanted antagonism.

When Charlie Dent, the loud mouthed villain said in a loud voice intended for everyone else to hear

"There's a hell of a smell of pigs in here" much to the raucous laughter of his family and friends, he was not expecting the retort from one of the younger officers who was walking past his table returning from the toilet.

"That's probably 'cos there is some shit on the seats" he responded equally as loud and in the purposeful direction of Charlie.

There were a couple of stifled sniggers from the younger officers, but a stunned stony silence from the rest of the birthday party. Charlie made half an effort to get up from his chair but a couple of the more sensible members of his family held him down.

It only took seconds, but the hairs were up on the back of most of the officers' necks, the conversation picked up slowly between the wives and partners and everyone tried to return to the party atmosphere. The seeds of doubt had once again been sown, was it not possible for them to go out as a group without some have a go hero spoiling it for them?

Seats were turned so that direct eye contact with Charlie and his crowd could not be made, at least not by anyone who knew him and the meal continued.

Fortunately Charlie's crowd finished their meal, but as they left there were the deliberate snorting sounds of pigs from nowhere in particular, which generated much amusement amongst the outgoing crowd. Glances around the table made sure that nobody rose to the taunt and the departing group all left the premises.

I silently prayed that they would not be going to the nightclub nearby, and fortunately they headed off in the opposite direction. After all, we were human and after a few beers even the best behaved could crack under duress.

After a wonderful meal and numerous drinks the meeting in the restaurant came to an end. Several of the older members would not be going onto the night club so they said their farewells and headed off home.

I was pleased to see that the rain had stopped; we were planning on going to the nightclub but didn't want a soaking.

It was very interesting to see how the door staff would react as the group approached. Many people never recognise officers out of uniform, and you could see some slow cogs turning as the bouncers joined the dots to realise there was a group of off duty officers coming in.

It was heaving. There were long queues at the bar, and absolutely no chance of the group staying together.

As could be expected the younger element launched onto the dance floor along with, by now, some slightly merry police wives. "It was good to see everyone enjoying themselves" I thought as I settled against a pillar along the back wall, once again I seemed to be lumbered with watching the drinks for everyone else.

The club was throbbing to the music, I had given up trying to have any form of shouted conversation above the music and relied on gestures and hand signals to communicate with the others. The dance floors were packed and it took forever to get to the bar or the toilet.

Just as I was returning to my drink a commotion to the right caught my eye. Two lads having a scrap right at the back, there was no chance that the bouncers could possibly see it. As my instinct took over I saw with respect that two of the shift jumped in to split it up, but the aggressor just kept on going on.

It was then that I realised in the gloom of the coloured lights that one of my mates who was trying to restrain this wild eyed young man was no other than Brian Collins, a time served officer who was presently off sick recovering from an embarrassing operation and he should definitely not be exerting himself!!

I couldn't see any sight of the bouncers, so I quickly pushed my way across to help Brian.

"My god" I thought as we attempted to wrestle the guy to the floor in a restraining arm lock "this guy must be on something, he doesn't feel pain!"

As we got the young lad pinned down he continued kicking and thrashing, I was aware of blood coming from somewhere but not sure where. It was not safe to hold him where he was, so as I tried telling the lad that I was a police officer and he was under arrest, another of the crew came to my help to lift him and get him to the exit. We were halfway across the dance floor by the time the bouncers arrived, but instead of us letting him go we just shouted for them to clear the way.

Very quickly we were outside the emergency exit which was hurriedly closed behind us. I realised with dismay that it had started raining again. The bouncers had their raincoats on. The silence outside was a remarkable contrast to the noise inside, and I tried to tell the young guy that I was going to ease up on the arm lock and to calm down, he just erupted again in a mass of flailing punches and kicks. The nearest bouncer kicked his legs from under him, and I quickly subdued him again.

"Call the van" I shouted to the bouncer, "he knows we're police."

"OK" came the reply and within a very short period of time the blue flashing lights of the town patrol van came swinging round the corner into the far reaches of the car park.

"Good luck with that one" said the bouncer in a knowing sort of way as the lad was led into the van still kicking and screaming.

I thought it was a slightly odd thing to say but didn't pay much attention to it. I conferred quickly with the van driver, telling him it was a straight forward arrest for breach of the peace, take him in, let him sleep it off and he could go in the morning with a caution.

It was agreed that the officer would take on the arrest and leave me out of the paperwork. With that the van pulled away and I decided, now wet and with blood on my shirt, that I had better get back inside and find Angela.

At least with the dim lighting I wouldn't look too out of place with the other sweaty bodies!

I found Angela who had heard about the fight. She was concerned when she saw the blood smears, but a quick check showed no cuts on me. We had just settled back into the party atmosphere when a call was made over the DJ's speakers system "could Tom Springfield go to the main door, Tom Springfield to the main door."

"What the hell now" I thought.

As I got to the door I saw the police van driver standing there with an apologetic look on his face.

"Sorry Tom, the Rottweiler won't accept the arrest from me. She wants you to come to the station to make a statement."

"Bugger" I thought "the bitch!" The Rottweiler was the nickname for the stony faced female "by the book" custody sergeant on duty in the bridewell that night. As she was on the opposite shift I had only had brief dealings with her, but knew she seemed to revel in flexing her authority and making hard work for others.

It was supposed to be a happy night out. It must be about one in the morning now, pouring with rain.

"OK, I'll just tell the missus, back in a second."

I pushed my way through the crowds, found Angela and made my apologies. I arranged for her to go home with another couple and went back to the entrance.

"Your mate got another shout and had to dash off" said the doorman.

"By the way, do you know who that lad is that you locked up?"

"Haven't got a clue" I said honestly.

"Only the son of the local MP, that's all" said the doorman with a belly laugh.

Now the previous comment made sense, and only now did I see why the Rottweiler was going to insist that every i was dotted and t crossed.

No taxis on the rank, I was already wet, so what the hell, only ten minutes walk to the nick, so I took off as quickly as I could.

I arrived at the front door reception area of the station. In front of me were a very well dressed couple obviously returning from a very posh night out, definitely matching the gleaming Bentley parked conspicuously in the front visitors car park.

The duty officer behind the desk activated the security lock and let me into the station area without a word.

I buzzed to be let in to the cell area and walked into the usual night time mayhem to be met with a very sombre faced custody sergeant.

"Good morning Sarge" I said as carefully as I could, well aware that I had had a few drinks and trying not to slur any words.

"Just look at the state of you" she sneered. I glanced sideways at my reflection in the darkened windows. I was wet, dripping in fact, the blood was running further into my white shirt, and I must have smelled of alcohol.

"Do you realise who you've locked up?" she snarled.

"Somebody said it was a big wig's son" I offered in an offhand manner, "but you can see he was well out of order and obviously on something more than just booze."

"Can't we just tell" she said, nodding her head towards the line of cell doors further down the corridor. One occupant in particular was not taking well to having been locked up. He was kicking and punching the steel door for all he was worth, screaming obscenities at the top of his voice.

"Is that him in five?" I asked with a grin.

"Sure is, and when he calms down he will be facing more than a breach of the peace. He kicked the police van causing damage and injured someone as they got him into the cell."

"Not only that, but Mummy and Daddy are at the front desk demanding to see their loving son. I told them they would have to wait for the arresting officer to turn up. It's all yours!"

"Oh boy" I thought "I bet this is the first time they have ever seen the inside of a police station, let alone a cell."

I made my way out to the front desk and opened the security door.

The lady in the posh fur coat looked at me as if I was something unwanted that she had stepped in on the pavement.

"Mr & Mrs Trowell?" I asked expectantly.

The man jumped to his feet as if the seat had been on fire.

"Not you? You're not the one who arrested him surely? You are no better than the rest of the yobs out there!"

"I am not here to argue" I said confidently. "I understand that you have been given special permission to see your son, which is most unusual."

"My friend the Chief Constable will hear about this first thing in the morning. You will be out of a job by lunchtime" boomed Mr Tony Trowell MP.

"I must warn you, your son is in an excitable state."

"Well, wouldn't you be, being locked up like a common criminal in this hell hole." boomed Mr Trowell.

As we were buzzed into the holding area we could hear the commotion coming from cell number five. The smell of vomit pervaded our nostrils and the assorted noises from elsewhere within the area created quite a racket.

"My God, what sort of animals have you got in here" Mrs Trowell said in an air of haughty disdain.

I grinned inwardly as I nodded to the Rottweiler to pass me the cell keys.

"Is it OK for them to see their son Sarge?" I asked respectfully.

"Just use the hatch and take care" she said with an evil grin.

I led the couple across to the line of cells, but then the haughty smirks on their faces fell as they stopped outside cell number five, the name "Trowell" written clearly in chalk on the board outside, as the door rattled under the constant barrage of kicks and punches and the nonstop filthy verbal onslaught coming from within.

I opened the spy hole, standing well back just in case a pointed finger or other undetected sharp object was pushed through.

"Trowell" I snapped "you have a visitor."

I slid back the bolt on the feeding flap. Mrs Trowell bent down in anticipation to see her dearly beloved "never do anything wrong "son.

Just then, as I had anticipated, and I guessed the custody officer had as well, there was a deep guttural sound from inside the cell as the occupant filled his mouth with as much phlegm as he could, to be launched with full force at whosoever dared to put their face in the space of the hatch.

I stood sideways and dropped the hatch, just as Mrs Trowell bent down to be greeted with a mouthful of slimy mucus and phlegm launched from the mouth of her wonderful son which landed square between her eyes.

She gasped in astonished horror and indignation. The son gazed out onto the one face in this world that he would never have expected to see and fell immediately silent. As the phlegm dripped from her face, Mr Trowell senior's unusually pale face seemed to regain colour. He took one look at his wife, another at his son, and then angrily slammed the inspection hatch shut and roared:

"Lock him up and throw away the key!" as he passed his wife a handkerchief and half marched, half dragged her out to the exit.

Nothing needed to be said as I showed them the way out.

"I wonder if my job will still be there on Monday" I mused inwardly as I returned to the interview room to write out my statement.

Amazingly the sound from number five stopped.

Chapter Five

Pedalling as fast as I could, I was trying to make up for lost time as I raced down to work. It had been a quick changeover from night shift to two/ten afternoons. It was always bad enough getting to sleep as the kids were up and about getting ready for school, but add that to the noisy bin men and a wrong number on the telephone, it was a recipe for disaster.

Still, the slowly falling light rain was fresh on my face and if I needed anything else to wake me up then that was just the thing, after I had committed the cardinal sin and "rolled over" for just another five minutes. I would make it, but not in my normal half hour comfort zone.

As I dashed in to the locker room there was an expectant buzz going round, something about young teenage wannabe's going out with the troops. Apparently one was an extremely attractive young lady and all the young studs were vying to see who she would be partnered with.

This was a first time initiative to show potential recruits what it was like on front line policing. Special permission and insurance had been obtained for them to accompany active units out and about, and perhaps shatter the TV image they may have had about the job.

I quickly got changed and went to get my radio, passing a few teenagers in the corridor, most unusual! I noted that I was on an area car beat, at last I could get some chasing paperwork done between jobs, and I would be out of the rain.

Entering the parade room I saw a group of seven teenagers, two girls and five lads standing at the front looking a little apprehensive. Inspector John Clegg came in and introduced them as potential recruits who had been given permission to come out with the crew. They were in no way to become involved in any policing matter and were there to observe only.

I thought that was a crazy idea. If any of the yobs saw one of them getting out of a police car they would immediately jump to the wrong conclusion, but, if the bosses had said yes then who was I to argue? The Inspector carried on to say that they were only there for the first half of the shift as they had done morning familiarisation with the dog and mounted sections.

"What a copout" I thought, "give them the fluffy world of the animals first, they certainly would not have seen them in the working environment which was quite a different matter."

The Inspector then began calling out the numbers of the officers and which teenager had been allocated. Just as I paid attention my number was called, and to the frustration of all the younger lads, the attractive brunette put up her hand to indicate her name and identity.

I got a quick playful poke in the ribs with the comment "safe in your hands then Tom!"

As it happens I was just about old enough to be her father if I had started young, and I suspected there was method in the madness as to why the Inspector had put us together. The rest of the briefing was completed and I made my way over to introduce myself.

"Hi, I'm Tom Springfield and you have got the short straw to double up with me for the afternoon!" I said with a smile.

"Hello, I'm Jenny Marsh," she replied with a gentle handshake. Her accent was not local and she spoke with a well educated soft voice.

"She may be a bit shy, but she'll need to toughen up if she wants to join the force" I thought to myself.

"Right then, let's see what the afternoon has got in store. If you're ready we can go out to the car." I noted she only had a smart black leather jacket, and was wearing jeans, but carried a small umbrella.

A quick check of the car, everything seemed OK and we both got in. The beauty of taking over a beat patrol is that the car is already warm, so there was no problem with steamed up windows from damp clothing like there would be in a cold car.

I explained the rules and emphasised that if we attended any incident where she was not comfortable, then she must just stand back and observe. We edged out into the slow moving traffic, it was a rainy autumn afternoon on market day, so there was a little bit more traffic than usual.

As I made my way to a central point of the beat and parked up so we could have a chat, I told her she could ask any questions she liked about the job and I promised to answer each one as honestly as I could. It turned out she was very impressed with the dog section and wanted to do that if she joined.

I smiled inwardly, just what I had expected. I tried to be positive, but explained that she would need to do a full two years probation before being considered, and it was pretty much dead men's shoes to get in. She appreciated that but was sure she would manage.

When I asked her why she wanted to join the force it quickly became apparent that her opinion was formed from the popular TV image and something else . . . .

"Forgive me for asking, but who's idea was it for you to apply?" I asked cautiously, as I had sensed that there may be more than just a little bit of parental pressure.

Her cheeks flushed a little as she played nervously with the zipper on her jacket.

"Well, my Dad is in the job and he thinks it would be ideal for me."

"Oh, I see. Where is he based, maybe I know him?"

She took a bit of a gulp before she answered quietly,

"He is a Chief Superintendent in the Met."

"Ah, I see, no chance of anyone knowing him out here in the sticks then!" I laughed.

"Please don't tell anyone," she pleaded, "I don't want any special treatment."

"That's fine by me" I said, thinking to myself that whether she liked it or not, if she joined the job and it got out, life could and would be different. There would be those who think she would get a helping hand every step of the way, and there would be those who would make life as difficult as they could for her.

"Hee hee" I thought, "maybe the young lads might not be in such a rush to get her phone number now!"

"I need to do some follow up enquiries first of all; it is the never ending battle with the paperwork. It is not glamorous but needs to be done." I explained.

I managed to get a couple of firearms application checks done and was just completing one witness statement when I got a call to a burglar alarm activation just around the corner from where we were on one of the posh estates.

Driving quickly but safely I raced down the suburban streets. I explained to Jenny that I had the blue lights switched on, but the vehicle was not fitted with two tone horns. If it had been I would not have used them just in case it was a burglary in progress and a delayed silent alarm activation, I didn't want the culprits alerting.

Arriving swiftly at the address, I could see a short gravelled driveway leading to the detached residence set in its' own grounds. There was a white van parked with doors opened reversed up to the garage, and I made a point of pulling up across the front of the van to block any escape.

I jumped out of the car as a very bewildered man appeared at the side, and before he had chance to say anything the shrill burglar alarm started to sound in the garage and the house, I had been right when I had expected a delayed activation.

The concerned look on the man's face and lack of any urgency to run away told me that things were maybe not what they seemed. I saw the writing on the side of the van, "Elmhurst Plumbers," a local firm I had heard of before. I motioned to the van driver to come round the side away from the noise.

"I don't believe it" said the driver, "she told me it would be OK to drop some gear off and leave it in the garage." He showed me a delivery docket with the correct address on, and I could see that indeed the guy was unloading rather than loading his van. I quickly called control to cancel any other units attending, and asked for a key holder to be notified.

If ever you have seen a police car racing past with lights and sirens going, to then pull off into a side road and turn them off, it is more than likely someone who has been answering a call, but received just such a cancellation from the first unit at the scene.

The key holder was contacted and on her way, and then the audible alarms stopped, leaving just the blue light flashing on the alarm box. "At least it is a new one" I said, "the old ones just keep on going!"

"Well, a little bit of excitement for you" I grinned as I noticed Jenny stood by the car looking a bit out of place. I told the plumber to carry on unloading, if he didn't need to stay then the key holder could just reset the system with the garage door closed, provided he didn't need to be in again that day.

Sure enough, he had just left as the key holder arrived; she was the sister of the householder who lived a couple of streets away. I quickly explained what had happened and asked her to check with her sister to make sure that the same thing didn't happen again.

It had just begun to darken down into that long dusk period when grey skies made the afternoon darker a lot earlier. The school run had started and the roads began to get crowded as that then merged into rush hour. It was pointless trying to move around for the hell of it, and I decided, as it was too dull to do paperwork in the car, that we would park up yet again and watch the world go by.

I explained to Jenny that just the visible presence by the roadside, where drivers could see they were being monitored, resulted in people double checking to see if they had their seat belt on, and checking their speed. I would also be watching for cars mentioned in the briefing, for obvious offences and for known criminals. Information was passed back to the liaison officer if a known villain was seen to be driving a new set of wheels, and also whom, if anyone, they were in the company of.

Just then a call went up for all units, anyone near the Lonsdale Hotel, serious accident nearby. I knew the traffic unit had been on the outskirts of town earlier dealing with another accident and were obviously not clear yet. I was about half a mile away and called in to see if I could be of any assistance. All the other units were busy, and I was allocated the job.

It was a farce not having the two tone horns I explained to Jenny as I started the car, put on the blue lights and started to head in the direction as quickly and as safely as I could.

As I pulled onto the main road I could see stationary traffic ahead. Fortunately the small patrol car came into its' own, because of its' size I could squeeze through gaps which perhaps the larger van might struggle to get through. I still had to use my horn a lot to attract the attention of drivers sat, windows closed, radio on; staring into space wondering what was causing the hold up.

Coming up to the main junction at the traffic lights I could see it was gridlocked, all traffic in front of me was stopped, and crossing traffic could not get through as the idiots went into the yellow hatch marking with no exit.

Nosing the police car gently into the junction, the blue lights reflecting off the nearby shop windows making it look like there were several blue light vehicles attending the scene, I had no choice but to edge up the middle of the road. As I got to the crest of the hill I could see ahead that traffic was clear about two hundred yards ahead, just past the pelican crossing.

There was a crowd of people at the side of the road, but no apparently damaged vehicles. It was then that I saw a figure lying in the road with people bent over it. I also saw a truck pulled over half on and half off the verge, hazard warning lights on, and I was just in time to see a male person leaning against the back of the truck apparently being violently sick.

There was nowhere else to go than to put the car in the middle of the road. Traffic could get past each side, and it would protect the scene. As I called in to say I was at the scene, I checked to make sure that an ambulance had been despatched and was on its way.

I knew the difficulty I had experienced getting through, and the ambulance was probably going to be coming from that same direction, so didn't hold out much hope for an early arrival, but at least they would have their sirens.

I quickly established the casualty was alive, and that the people tending him were two passing nurses and a doctor. Blood was mingling with the rainwater and trickling down the street, the elderly male casualty obviously had head and leg injuries.

As always at the scene of an accident, I made sure that I was wearing a high visibility jacket, protect yourself, then the scene. I confirmed to the helpers that an ambulance was on its' way, and gave a blanket from the boot of the car to cover him, heaven knows what difference it would make, he was lying on a road in the pouring rain in mid autumn.

Witnesses were always a treasure and I quickly found several, all whom gave the same account, the casualty had attempted to cross the busy road some seventy yards beyond the pelican crossing, but stepped out into the path on the oncoming truck. The driver never stood a chance of stopping.

It also became apparent that the guy I had seen throwing up at the back of the truck was in fact the driver, very much in shock. I had a quick word with him to check he was OK, and then asked if he could just move the truck off the road into the hotel car park, as we really needed to do something about this rush hour traffic as the ambulance would be trying to get through.

I quickly marked the road where I could see the skid marks, and reluctantly had to make a mark around where the casualty still lay. They dare not move him just yet.

"Where on earth is that ambulance" I thought, but just then detected the distinctive wailing banshee siren in the distance.

I arranged with Pete in the control room to contact the lorry drivers' company to send out another driver, fortunately he was just returning to the depot which was not too far away, but he was not in any fit state to drive any further than the car park.

The attending doctor and nurses were concerned about the casualty. One of the nurses told me that he was drifting in and out of consciousness, but they were getting worried as he was getting so cold. His injuries may prove fatal. On hearing that I radioed for more assistance and was relieved to hear that the traffic unit was clear of the other job, they would be attending and were coming in from the clear side of town.

Rubber Neckers were making it very difficult for me to get the traffic moving out of town. I had to relieve some of the congestion from the crossroads further up to give the ambulance a chance. As the sound of the ambulance sirens got closer, I became aware of another sound, the two tone horns of the traffic car coming from the other direction, the cavalry were coming!

Both units arrived at the same time, and as is inevitable traffic clogged up again as the two extra vehicles had nowhere to go. I quickly briefed the traffic officers who needed to take a few measurements straight away as the marks on the road would soon be rubbed off in the rain and traffic.

The casualty was carefully lifted onto a stretcher, and just as he was being placed in the ambulance I asked him his name, and where he lived. It turned out he lived just around the corner and had been going to the fish and chip shop.

"Is there anyone at home" I asked quickly.

"Just Milly," came the answer, "who's going to look after her?" he said in a concerned voice.

"Who's Milly?" I asked urgently, but Cyril Benson had slipped back unconscious again.

The ambulance cleared away from the scene, the necessary measurements were taken, so I pulled my car up onto the kerb. One of the traffic officers was collecting further witness details, as the other was speaking to the lorry driver who was now in the patrol car.

As I bent down to recover the now sodden and blood soaked blanket from the road, I had an awful feeling of having forgotten something.

Paperwork OK, equipment OK, what on earth was it?

Just then I caught sight of a very cold wet figure huddled under a small umbrella wearing a black leather jacket and jeans.

"Oh, hell, I'd forgotten all about her" I thought. When I got over to Jenny she was trembling, not only from the cold but from what she had just witnessed.

"We need to get you back to the station" I said, "but there is one more little job I need to do," I said apologetically.

"I've missed my train" said Jenny, "no rush."

I drove quickly round the corner to the address given by Cyril. I told Jenny to stay in the car and get warmed through. There were no lights on inside, and no reply to my loud knocking. I decided a check next door was required, and knocked loudly.

The elderly lady who answered the door looked surprised and worried; having a policeman on the doorstep was never going to be good news!

"Sorry to bother you, but I am trying to contact next door. I'm afraid Cyril has had an accident, but he was concerned for Milly. Can you tell me who she is and where she might be?"

As if in answer to my question, there was a loud miaow from the top of garden fence, the old lady pointed with a shaky crooked finger and said "there she is!"

The penny dropped, Milly was his cat.

I asked politely if she knew of any relatives and took details including an address the old lady provided, thanking her profusely.

Opening the car door, I was just about to get in when I received a call from control.

The hospital had been in touch, Cyril didn't make it.

Traffic would deal with the accident report, could I attend for the sudden death procedure?

Jenny heard all this and started sobbing uncontrollably. I wasn't sure what to say or do, so quietly drove back to the station to drop her off.

"So, it turned out to be quite a day" I said as we walked across the car park, "now what do you think to front line policing?"

"Never, no way, it's not for me, I don't care what Dad says!" came the fierce reply.

"At least she has found a bit of backbone and the bubble has been burst" I thought as I bid farewell and went for a bite to eat before attending the hospital for the sudden death enquiries.

Chapter Six

Early on at the beginning of the nightshift, the rain began to fall. For a Thursday the town centre was surprisingly full of people, at least I would not be bored.

The rain tended to make people dash from pub to pub, not hanging around on the streets talking. As the night went on the more intoxicated people became, they seemed to become immune to the rain and once soaked through, just accepted it.

Whilst not wanting to be labelled a voyeur or similar, it intrigued me why dress sense came before common sense. The lack of clothing was astounding. OK, some of the ladies out for the night may have the figures to show off, but many others didn't, but nobody seemed to have told them.

The "girls", and in that term I could cover the mutton dressed as lamb up to fifty year olds, would come out wearing only the skimpiest of outfits, hardly warm enough on a tropical beach never mind the rainy streets of Denby in autumn.

Why on earth didn't they wear a substantial coat? How come they were always taken by surprise when they had to queue outside in the rain and cold to get into clubs, and later at taxi ranks to get home?

I shook my head slowly as another group of giggling women tottered between pubs. As the night rolled on their fancy hair do's and makeup would deteriorate along with their demeanour.

"Lights" I heard shouted from down the street. As I looked up I noticed a posh car coming towards me the wrong way down the one way system without lights. Someone had tried to shout the warning to the driver. I strode out into the road indicating for the vehicle to stop, always ready for a final jump if they failed to see me or plain didn't want to stop.

A vehicle being driven without lights was a good indication of a drink driver.

I also noticed the driver of the dark coloured BMW was not wearing a seat belt either as I directed the car into the safety of a bus lay by and bent down to speak to the driver.

An awful smell of stale alcohol and rich spicy food oozed out of the now open driver side window.

"Good evening Officer" greeted the suave young man wearing a cravat and expensive shirt.

"Good evening Sir, are you a stranger to the town?" I asked politely as the rain dripped off my helmet, narrowly missing going inside the car.

"Well, yes I am actually, how did you know?" he replied in a very well spoken voice.

"It was probably something to do with the fact that you were travelling the wrong way on a one way street."

"Oh bother, can I get turned round here?" he asked innocently.

"Well you could, but I believe you may have been drinking as you were driving without lights and I can smell alcohol on your breath. I am going to ask you to provide a road side breath test."

I called on the radio giving my exact location and one of the highly visible traffic cars quickly arrived. The test showed a positive reading immediately so the man was arrested and placed in the back of the car.

It meant that I would have to drive the BMW back to the nick.

It took me a while to get used to the cockpit style layout in the driving seat; my first impressions were not good. "If this is luxury they can stick it" I thought to myself.

I found the light switches and wipers and took my time to swing the car round to point in the right direction and follow the traffic car back to the station.

When I came to deal with my prisoner, I was amazed to find that when he turned out his pockets he had no money on him at all. His wallet was filled with various plastic cards, but no cash.

"How the other half live" I thought.

To everyone's annoyance the main breath testing machine failed during its self checking procedure. The readings were way out. They tried to reboot it and try once more; still readings came up outside acceptable limits. That meant it would be necessary to call the police doctor to take a blood sample, which often took time at this hour of the night.

The car driver turned out to be an accountant. He claimed to have only drunk a couple of pints, but the speed of the road side test indicator told me a different story. When asked if there was any reason why he would not be able to give blood he shook his head, so the custody sergeant informed him that the doctor was already on his way.

I was aware that if a driver was only marginally over the limit, any delay in getting him tested may result in the alcohol clearing his system sufficiently to scrape through. An agonising half hour crept passed waiting for the doctor to arrive.

The driver had requested, in his posh voice, not to be placed in a cell. He said he had claustrophobia and it might bring on a panic attack. Although the interview room did not have any windows he felt OK to stay in there in the knowledge that the door would not be locked.

Anything to make life easier and avoid a high level complaint, heaven knows who he may have contacts with in the world of money and power, we decided to let him stay in the interview room which was not required at the moment, and the rest of the cell area was secure.

Another prisoner not so polite or calm was also waiting in one of the cells for the doctor to arrive. He would be seen first as his time of arrest had been fractionally earlier.

At last the doctor arrived and quickly set about taking a blood sample from the first prisoner. Once done I went to get my prisoner from the interview room. I pointed him in the direction of where the doctor was standing, and as I was behind him I did not see the colour drain from the prisoners face.

The doctor had turned round with a hypodermic needle in his hand. The prisoners' hand shot to his mouth but, too late. Whatever exotic food and drink he had consumed on his night out spewed out through his fingers going everywhere. The doctor jumped back to avoid the splashing mess, but the smell!!!

Unfortunately a cell area is not the sort of place you can just open the windows and doors to let fresh air in. Having prisoners puking in the cells was kind of expected, but they did have a toilet to try to hit, and the smell tended to stay confined as the positive pressure system drew the fumes away.

The main bridewell area was a different matter.

Obviously the custody sergeant had the priority of getting it cleaned up, and as the unwritten rule goes, he who did it mopped it up!

I didn't want to tread on his toes, but the clock was ticking and it had been nearly an hour since the arrest, I needed that sample. It turned out the prisoner was not only claustrophobic but he had a fear of needles as well.

This was a new one to me; I wasn't sure where I stood.

"I asked you if there was any reason why you couldn't give a blood sample and you never said anything" I snorted at the prisoner who now had a mop in his hand.

"Sorry, I never thought that bit out" he murmured, appalled at having to clean up his own mess.

The doctor was of the opinion that he should be OK giving a sample, but the custody officer could see complaints in big lights if they tried to force him. Talk about "cover your arse."

The prisoner had heard this and immediately picked up on the fact that he could not be forcefully required to give a blood sample.

"OK" I said, "now we go for the urine then."

The benefit of the prisoner having been in the interview room was that there had not been a toilet, so I knew with reasonable certainty that he would be ready.

The container was given to the prisoner and I escorted him to the toilet. Of necessity I needed to stand behind him just in case the guy tried to scoop water out of the toilet into the sample jar or any other dodge. Listening to him having a pee made me want to go but that would have to wait.

As the prisoner turned around and appeared to be attempting to put the lid on the container, his hands suddenly jerked and he dropped the container and contents onto the floor.

I was speechless.

Had that really been an accident, or was this guy literally taking the piss out of the system??

I was fuming, I had been lulled into a false sense of security all along, and now my case appeared to be growing wings.

I stormed back to the custody desk, half dragging my charge with me.

"He spilled it!" I nearly spat the words out.

The custody officer responded with his been there, done that, seen it all attitude, casually walked to the waiting mop and bucket, pushed it into the hands of the very sheepish prisoner and pointed him towards the toilet.

"Right, as I see it this is going down as a 'fail to provide'." the custody officer said.

"He has had his chances and blew it. If we detain him to wait for another urine sample we can't watch him so he could off load in the toilet in the cell. Plus if we put him in the cell and he has a panic attack he may end up in hospital so we don't get another sample. The time frame is getting too long, and I'm certainly not having him in the interview room."

The doctor quickly filled in his relevant paperwork, the mop and bucket was locked away so as not to be an available weapon for any prisoners coming in later.

The prisoner was charged with failing to provide a sample for analysis. His car would be held in the back yard until morning and the prisoner was released. He had no coat, no paper money and was in a strange town, I really couldn't give a flying fart whether he was inconvenienced or not. I had an awful feeling that a good brief would get this one off.

Still. If I looked on the brighter side of things, I had been out of the rain for a while.

As I was in and it was close to early meal break, I decided to have a bite now rather than coming back later.

Refreshed and fed I made my way out onto town. The rain had stopped and there were more people out on the streets, those not going clubbing were making their way home.

I met up with another couple of foot patrols making their way back for their break. They said everything seemed quiet and were about to head off when we all heard a screech of tyres from around the corner.

As we looked in the direction of the noise we saw a car at an angle across the road, apparently having swerved to avoid a youth walking in the road. A bit of verbal was being exchanged when, to our amazement, the youth who had narrowly missed being mown down stormed across to some nearby road works and pulled up one of the iron bars used to hold the plastic red and white warning tapes.

He then swung it round his head and headed for the still stationary car.

Without warning he brought it crashing down onto the bonnet, yet another swipe at the windscreen. The driver of the car floored it to get away as the youth looked for another target. I had seen enough and ran across to stop the youth who saw me coming and began to run away, still carrying the bar. I didn't really stop to think about it, but just kept chasing. If the youth had stopped and confronted me with the bar, I knew I might have a problem.

The chase turned into a dimly lit side street and with a gigantic effort I launched myself into a crushing rugby tackle onto the youth. The bar flew sideways and I landed with a sickening crunch on top of the youth, clearly knocking the wind out of him, but I was not sure if I had hurt myself in the process.

At times like this the adrenaline is flowing and pain does not always register initially.

I quickly got the handcuffs on the stunned youth and arrested him for criminal damage and possession of an offensive weapon. I collected my hat, and with the youth in one arm and the iron bar in the other marched him back to the scene. I was quietly proud of this arrest, the other two officers although big and burly would not have had my turn of speed, and I noticed that they didn't make any effort to join the chase.

The car driver had stopped further up the road and was being spoken to by the other officers. To see me marching the offender proudly back to the scene they knew another detected crime was going to be notched up.

The driver and the youth did not appear to know each other so it was not a premeditated attack, just a drunken spur of the moment thing. Because it had been my arrest I escorted the youth back in the van, only one of the other bobbies could come in for his scheduled break as I was dealing with the prisoner, they needed another body out on the streets.

As the adrenaline began to ease down I became aware of intense pain around my left ribcage and left leg. I noticed my shin was grazed and bleeding, but as I straightened up I struggled to catch my breath as pain seared through my chest. Colin Shepherd the custody sergeant saw the pain wracked features as I stood up.

"Are you OK Tom?" he queried. "Do you want me to put an injury on duty entry in the log?"

Normally I wouldn't bother with such things. I would just shrug it off and carry on.

Something made me think twice this time, "Yeah, I think we better had" I said.

After processing the prisoner who was considered too drunk to interview, I filled in my pocket book and made a quick statement. I obtained the car owner details from my colleague and would need to arrange for a statement later. I found I was really struggling to get comfortable and as time went on it became painful when I breathed.

"You'd better get checked out" Colin said as he could see I was in a lot of discomfort.

"Casualty at this time should have quietened off, get yourself over there now" he advised.

"OK Sarge" I grudgingly agreed.

I got a lift to casualty and let the control room know I would be off radio for a while.

Many times I would call in at the nurse's station for a cuppa, so when I turned up it came as no great surprise. When I said I needed checking out they originally thought I was joking, but as I winced when I turned they saw that I wasn't kidding.

The casualty area was quiet so I received VIP treatment and was soon pressing my chest against the cold plates of the X-ray machine. "Turn around and one for luck from the back" instructed the attractive radiologist who I believed to be the wife of an officer on the opposite shift, whom I didn't know so well.

Back in the cubicle as I got dressed and waited for the doctor to review the X-ray I began thinking if I really wanted to continue doing this job. How many other people go to work in the knowledge that they may become injured by the end of the day?

I also knew I was my own worst enemy. I noticed the "uniform carriers" out there who did just enough to get by never seemed to get injured. Then again, they would go off work with a sniffle or a cold, I could never do that. If I didn't get stuck in so readily I could avoid these lumps and bumps.

The arrival of the doctor broke into my thoughts.

"Let's have a look" she said as the fluorescent light board flickered on.

She slid the X-rays into the retaining clips and looked closely.

"Oh yes, look there, there and there" she pointed to three places.

Even to my untrained eye I could see three distinct areas which did not have the smooth lines of the other bones.

"You have a couple of cracked ribs" she said. "They are not displaced so don't appear to be a potential problem, but your whole ribcage area is likely to be bruised."

"We can strap you up for a bit of support, but I'm afraid it will just be a case of taking it easy for a while." She smiled.

"OK, thanks Doc" I said with a sigh.

At that time there was a discussion raging as to whether it was possible for an officer to be on duty yet also be on light duties. The PC brigade (as in politically correct) was arguing that any officer on duty in uniform should be available to do any job demanded of him or her. I couldn't see how that could apply to pregnant female officers, and anyway it was a great time to catch up on paperwork.

They checked my grazed shin and gave it a quick clean up bit didn't pay much more attention to it. I took advantage of the time to then have a cuppa and catch up on a bit of chat. They all knew I was married but flirted with me mercilessly; something unwritten about the uniform on both sides brings out the worst. I was flattered but never gave it another thought.

I arranged to be picked up and taken back to the station where the duty inspector had been advised of the injuries. Because they were necessarily self inflicted and not intentional criminal injuries he didn't seem too concerned. He told me to go home and see how I felt the following night.

If I felt up to it I could come in to do paperwork and maybe a control room relief. If not he would need a sick note if I wanted to take more time off.

"Jeeesus" I thought angrily, "some of those uniform carriers would milk this for weeks."

It was not something I would personally do.

"OK Sir thanks" yet I wondered why I was saying thanks for nothing in particular.

Just then I needed to cough and I suddenly remembered how much it hurt me to do so.

It was definitely time to go home, sod the paperwork, time for some well earned rest and recuperation. There comes a time when trying to help others just doesn't seem so attractive.

Chapter Seven

"How on earth have they managed that?" I wondered as I responded to a call to a car crash in the car park of the local high school.

It was a crisp autumn morning just after tea break as I travelled to the location. The call had come in from the head teacher as a matter of urgency, and I knew from previous dealings that it took a lot to get this man in a flap.

As I arrived it was easy to see the problem. A typical "boy racer" car, with go faster stripes and numerous additional headlights had wrapped the front end of his car around the security gate and pillar.

It was a slow speed area, no heavy traffic, so what had happened here?

I saw the headmaster standing with a sheepish looking youth who I instantly recognised was Tim Roberts, who, if I was not mistaken, was a disqualified driver.

So, what was the score?

The headmaster, Mr Humphreys, was beside himself with contempt and rage. He was only a short man, maybe five feet tall, shaped like a barrel, but he had a booming voice of which any sergeant major would have been proud.

He very quickly explained that the young man had been annoying everyone driving round the car park with his souped up motor which would emit a loud rallying sound as it slowed down. He had obviously been trying to impress some of the girls and maybe some lads with his antics, but the headmaster had warned him off twice.

It was as he approached him once more during the tea break that the youth had made one last run up the car park and managed to collide with the barrier, a hand operated red and white pole with counter balance mounted on a sturdy concrete base. The barrier was only in the down position after school hours, so had been up at the time of the collision.

My head was spinning. I was almost sure that the lad would not have insurance, but the car park, by having a barrier, would not be classed as a public highway. He must obviously have driven on a road to get to the school, and the fact that Tim Roberts was not too bright it would not be difficult to establish that, but I couldn't see him being covered for the damage.

"OK, Tim, what happened?" I asked, knowing full well that Tim would soon dig himself a deep hole as he always did.

"I was doing a few burn offs in the car park but as I was leaving the steering locked up."

(This indicated straight away that he had been driving the car.)

"What do you mean, burn offs?" I asked.

"If you get a bit of speed going and turn the ignition off, it begins to backfire" he explained enthusiastically.

"And didn't you realise that by turning the keys your steering lock would be likely to come on?" I asked somewhat sarcastically.

"It hadn't happened before" replied Tim puzzled.

I wondered if that might constitute reckless driving, but I would need to show that Tim had the ability to realise the result of his actions and that might be a problem.

"Whose car is it" I quizzed.

"Mine!" said Tim proudly.

If I was not mistaken Tim was behind on paying fines at court and was not employed.

"How did you manage to buy it" was the next question.

"I got a loan." The hole just got deeper!

"Have you got your licence back then?"

"Of course" Tim lied. It was painfully obvious to me that he was making a very bad attempt at lying his way out.

"I think we need to sort this out at the station. I'm arresting you on suspicion of driving whilst disqualified" I said as I cautioned him. Because I was by myself I handcuffed him and placed him in the back of the car.

I had a quick word with the headmaster. Recovery of the car would be delayed. I suspected that it had been obtained by deception but could not yet confirm that. I was sure Tim would not have any recovery cover, but if it was evidence in a crime it would be seized and returned to the holding compound.

I checked out the car, the engine fired up, so with a sickening screeching sound I delicately reversed it away from the barrier and up onto the grass area nearby.

I got the necessary contact details and drove back to the station, aware of the fact that Tim appeared to be wriggling awkwardly in the back seat. I reversed into the secure holding bay and waited for the shutter to close. I then got Tim out of the back and knowing the cameras were watching, I then searched around the back seat.

As expected I felt something down the back of the seat. I pulled it up to reveal three buff coloured empty wage packets.

As I got out of the car, I waved the envelopes in front of Tim's nose, very definitely for the benefit of the camera record. I had a pocketbook entry to say I had searched the vehicle at the beginning of the shift. As there had been no other rear seat passengers then anything found could be accurately linked to Tim.

I looked at the payslips, surprise surprise, made out to Danny Roberts, who I was sure would be Tim's older brother. A decent hard working lad, this was going to get messy.

I was sure that Tim was just a bit simple and not retarded. I checked with the Detective Inspector to make sure that it would be OK to interview him unattended. Previous dealings had never been challenged so he gave the green light to go ahead.

Once the original paperwork had been completed I let control room know that I was going to be out of action, so another officer took up the mobile beat patrol. I then started the interview with Tim.

The loan for six hundred pounds had been obtained at a local bank. As it happened Tim still had his copy of the agreement crumpled up in his pocket. It turned out he had just got the loan last night and picked up the car straight away paying cash.

He hadn't had time to get insurance but there was a valid tax disc and MOT.

I nearly asked if the bank were giving away driving licences but then realised my sarcasm may have been lost on Tim.

"So, what is the situation with your licence as last time I heard you were banned?"

"I only got a twelve month ban and that was last year" he replied confidently.

"But the ban goes from one date to another date; don't you know what that date is?" I asked.

"No, but if it was last year it will be gone by now."

I stopped the interview and called the control room for a drivers check which I realised perhaps I should have done in the first place, as that was the power of arrest used. Within seconds the results were relayed back to me, disqualified until November this year. That was still a few weeks away.

"Tell me about the loan" I asked as the interview resumed.

"It was really easy to get, my mate told me if I took in three wage slips and two utility bills I could get the money. I borrowed Danny's wage slips and Dads bills and it was sorted."

"But didn't you know it is illegal to pretend to be someone else to get money?" I queried.

"The Bank won't know."

"But what about paying the money back?"

"Well, I don't need to as they don't know who I am."

"And what happens when Danny gets a bill?" I continued.

"Well, he didn't get the money so why would he have to pay it back?" asked Tim.

If ever there was a simplistic explanation that just had to be it!

"So, you know it is wrong to pretend to be someone else to obtain money then." I confirmed.

"Well yes." Tim mumbled.

"And you knew you couldn't pay the money back?"

"Well, yes, sort of."

"What do you mean sort of?"

"I didn't think I would have to pay it back because they don't know who I am?"

I realised I was going round in circles. I told Tim that he was also under arrest for obtaining property by deception. I then closed the interview and put Tim in a cell after confirming where I could find Danny at work and which bank had given the loan.

It was just coming up to lunchtime and I struck lucky. I contacted Danny's workplace and yes he was due a break. He was only a short distance away and said he wouldn't mind coming to the police station as long as it didn't take long. I didn't tell him what it was about.

As I was waiting for him to arrive, I contacted the bank to make an appointment to speak with the manager. Yes, it was important. Yes it was a criminal matter. Yes, I would be in uniform.

"Ok, you may come in at one o'clock this afternoon." I was informed.

"Wow," thought I, "I'm supposed to be helping them!"

Danny arrived and was shown into the interview room. I needed to confirm that he knew nothing so had to tread carefully.

"Do you recognise these?" I asked as I passed the wage packets now contained in a plastic evidence bag across the desk.

"Blimey, they're mine, where did you find them?" he asked with a worried look on his face.

"When was the last time you saw them" was the next question.

"I always put them in my drawer in my bedroom." He groaned realising something was amiss.

"And who else has access to your room" I asked as coolly as possible.

"Oh come on, what is this? Unless someone broke in then it would be my family in the house."

"And you can confirm that your brother Tim lives with you." I said.

"I knew it, what the hell has he been doing now?"

I explained what had occurred, glad in the knowledge that Tim was in a cell and nowhere near his older brother! I had to explain that Danny would need to make a statement exonerating himself; otherwise if he tried to cover for his brother he could be considered an accessory and also charged with the deception.

He was fuming. He had kept his nose clean all this time whilst his runaway sibling was constantly in trouble, and now he had dragged him into it. Enough was enough.

"What do I write?" he asked.

I obtained the details I required and got the necessary signatures, thanking Danny as I led him outside. I then had chance to make a call to arrange recovery of the car, giving the keys to Mick in the van so they could pick it up easily before I dashed off to the bank.

The fact that I had the copy of the agreement with me made things go smoothly with the bank. They were always very strict on customer privacy but the situation as it was allowed them to provide a statement of complaint.

I tried hard to emphasise that the brother was in no way involved and that under no circumstances should any effort be made to contact him in relation to this loan, or to place any markers on his credit rating. I had promised Danny that I would do my best to make sure that he would not get any black marks against his record.

Technically the car would be the property of the bank after the court case, but I doubted they would recover their money, knowing the scrap man who collected those vehicles offered pennies for them and made a killing by providing his service.

All that was left to do was to charge Tim with the various offences and bail him to court. Knowing the history of non payment of fines I warned him that he would probably end up in custody. Previously he had been detained in a juvenile facility, this time he was in the big boys league, heaven help him!

Chapter Eight

The very nature of shift work meant that we often had to help out other colleagues to complete their enquiries. For example if they were just about to go on leave or were working nights and it was important, requests were made to do follow up enquiries on their behalf.

I had been allocated a foot beat in the residential area close to the sea front. There had been a serious incident the night before where a stabbing had taken place. The culprit had been caught, but seeing as CID officers were tied up with another major crime, I had been asked to obtain a witness statement.

The afternoon two to ten shift was always a good time for paperwork enquiries, normally a good time to find people at home.

I had plenty of work to cover of my own, but one more statement wouldn't be a problem. It was just as important to help my colleagues as to help the public. As it happened, the female officer dealing with the incident on night shift was a good friend having previously worked on our shift and we had worked well together.

Ms Glenda Quirke answered the phone with a very soft, sexy sounding voice and I was slightly taken aback at first. I explained that I had been asked to obtain her witness statement from the night before and would like to know a suitable time to call round. She indicated that five thirty would be good, so I agreed to try to be there by then, other duties permitting.

The details given were just a name and address. I had no idea who she may be, how old or young or anything else. The fact it said Ms on the message had me thinking she would be an elderly spinster of some sort.

I managed to complete other enquiries and had not received any additional duties, so just after five thirty I notified control that I would be out of action taking a statement, I then knocked on the door of number 35 Seacliffe Road.

The frosted glass in the front window blurred the view inside, but I could see movement as someone came to the door. As the door opened a very attractive lady in what I guessed would be her late thirties was revealed. With a smile I introduced myself and asked if she was in fact Glenda Quirke.

She responded with a beaming smile of perfect white teeth and full lips, inviting me into the hallway. Like any healthy male I always appreciated the sight of a beautiful woman, but being a family man never let my feelings get out of hand. This lady certainly seemed to have it all.

Her black curly hair shone in the available light, reaching halfway down her back. She was wearing a long sleeved skin tight white top with a plunging neckline, showing off magnificent breasts which were being supported by an uplift bra. Her blue jeans hugged her hips and she seemed naturally at ease in bare feet on the polished wooden floor. She only wore a slight hint of makeup.

My attention was then drawn to someone else just coming out of the kitchen. It was a bespectacled young lad with a spotty complexion, about fourteen years of age. When he saw me in uniform standing there he shot a quizzical look towards Ms Quirke.

"What's wrong Mum? I haven't done anything!" he was quick to say.

"It's nothing to do with you this time Stephen, it's about what happened last night. Here, go to the pictures or something and get something to eat in town," she said, passing him a ten pound note.

He didn't need telling twice and quickly grabbed his jacket and went out of the door.

"I am sure you would like a cup of tea or something" she purred in her seductive voice. Knowing that the statement may take some time I accepted the offer and the plate of biscuits which were served up at the same time were very tempting.

"Please, come into the living room, it is far more comfortable." She said.

As we entered the expensively decorated room she indicated for me to sit in the large armchair opposite the television which had a small coffee table alongside it. I had just sat down when she placed the tray with the two tea cups and biscuit plate onto the table.

I wasn't sure if it had been my imagination or not, but I am sure she lingered as she leaned over to place the tray, giving me a very close up view of her cleavage.

To my surprise, rather than sit elsewhere, she sat directly in front of the chair on the sheepskin rug. She knelt down in front of me, a slight smile on her face, what a beautiful picture of a woman she was. I started feeling a little uneasy at the whole situation.

Was she coming on to me, was she just being friendly, was I being set up? Whatever the case, my ethics kicked in and I tried to clear my mind for the purpose of my visit. She attempted to make some more small talk but I pulled out a blank statement form in an effort to be professional.

One of the first entries after name and address was the date of birth. When I delicately asked her age she smiled coyly and said;

"What do you think?"

Working on the basis that she had a fourteen year old son, I guessed at mid thirties.

"Oh you *are* kind" she smiled; she then gave her date of birth which in a quick reckoning made her forty eight years old.

"Wow," I thought, "I hope Angela looks as good as this when she's nearly fifty."

"Stephen is my third child, the others have left home. Since my husband died this house has begun to get a bit big for the two of us."

So, there it was, an apparently rich attractive widow living alone, ooooh the temptation!!

It was as if she had volunteered the information to let me know that no husband would be walking through the door after a day at the office, and I knew she had despatched the son into town. I noticed she still wore two rings.

"Would you please tell me everything you can about the incident last night, obviously I don't know what happened and need to hear everything you saw and heard."

She began to tell me how she had been woken up by screaming outside just after one o'clock in the morning. It had been a warm night so she had her front bedroom window open. She got up without putting a light on and peered out onto the street. She could see a young couple in their twenties arguing, the female seemed to be punching the male occasionally but he made no effort to retaliate. The young woman stormed off and the lad leaned against the lamp post and lit a cigarette. Ms Quirke made her way back to bed.

A couple of minutes later the shouting started again, then a couple of screams from the female and a frightening shout of pain from the male.

"You'll be sorry you ever met me!" screamed the girl. As Ms Quirke looked out again she was just in time to see something in the hand of the girl glint in the streetlight. The man was slumped on the floor by the lamp post clutching his chest.

It was then that she had dialled 999 and called for police and ambulance.

They arrived shortly afterwards and she had gone out to give a description to the attending female officer of the girl who had run off.

"OK, let's try to get some of that down on paper. Before we do, could you show me where you had been standing when you witnessed the scene, just to get an idea of your viewpoint and perspective." I said as routinely as possible.

"Of course, follow me" she said as she jumped to her feet. She led the way out of the room and up the stairs,

"Oh what a beautiful view that is" I thought as her hips swayed in front of me.

The front bedroom had an old style dressing table standing in a bay window. There was ample room to get past the end of the bed, but the side of the dresser where the open window had been was a bit narrow. Ms Quirke stood in the position where she had looked out onto the street.

"Look, you can see the lamp post from here" she said, pointing out of the window. From my position the mirror of the dressing table blocked my view.

"Squeeze in here and I'll show you!" she encouraged, pulling my arm closer to where she was standing. The fact that she was a buxom lady standing in a small space did not leave a lot of room for me.

As I tried to see the angle of view she had described, our bodies touched and it felt electric, I must have blushed as she said: "Mmm, this is nice" with a mischievous grin.

It would have just been so easy at that point to go with the flow, but alarm bells were ringing in my head. If I went ahead and followed my urges, the repercussions could be horrendous. She could claim rape, I would lose my job, my family and any good reputation I may have had. Was that worth it just for a few moments of madness?

I commented that the view outside was clear and close enough to be seen even at night, then made a hasty retreat to the landing and down into the living room.

Ms Quirke followed me down, but as I sat down I could see that she went to sit on the sofa in the corner, maybe I detected a bit of a pout in her moist lips. She had given up any attempts at flirting and just seemed to want to get the statement written and get me out of the house.

I quickly formulated the statement in the right sequence but wrote it down in her words, making sure all points of evidence had been covered. It was only as I asked her to sign it that I looked closely at her hands. They were perhaps the only part of her body to give a hint to her actual age.

As I got up to leave she said with a winsome smile:

"It was very nice to meet you, feel free to drop in anytime you are in the area for a cup of tea" It would have been just too easy to take her up on the offer. I said my goodbye and made my way back to the office.

"Close call boy, well done though," I said to myself.

Angela couldn't understand why I was more than my usual affectionate self when I returned home, and I didn't dare tell her. Some things are better left unsaid.

Chapter Nine

Sunday morning early shift was normally a quiet time to get on top of the never ending paperwork mountain. Traditionally it was bad form to go knocking on doors to get statements or do routine enquiries, so it was pretty much pushing paperwork.

There was always the jostle with others as to who could implore the duty sergeant best to be allowed to stay in the station, but for the others who were allocated a vehicle beat, provided they got themselves sorted out before they left the station, if they were lucky they could get parked up in a reasonably conspicuous spot to be seen, but they could actually catch up on paperwork.

The big danger to that was that if they received an urgent call, the temptation to throw everything together in a pile wrecked the file preparation layout and they were back where they started.

For whatever reason I was considered unflappable and being of slightly more mature years than the rest did not make as much noise when it came to desk time.

It came as no great surprise to find that I had been allocated foot beat in the town centre.

It was a crisp winter morning out there, not a lot going on, worse still, very few places open early for a morning cuppa.

My regular bakery didn't open on Sundays, but there was always the early café open for the fishermen going out on the river and then out to sea. It was always a question of timing with that one.

Depending upon the time of the tide dictated what time the small parties of day tripper fishermen began to congregate on the dockside.

The owner of the small café "Reel 'Em In" was always on top of the game, never missing a chance for sales. He knew on a cool morning many more than would fit in the café would be wanting something hot to drink and maybe a butty, so he had a side hatch open as well.

If I timed it right I could always get a cuppa just after the fishing groups left but before the holidaymakers got up.

Walking the empty streets, my footsteps echoing around the enclosed shopping area, a Sunday morning beat was considered very quiet. I could do a routine check on door handles as I went round, heaven forbid if I found something the night shift had missed.

There were no postmen out and about, and because it was winter the couple of street sweepers normally employed started a lot later, so not really anyone to pass the time of day with. Because so many of the small businesses did not open on Sundays, if they had had unwelcome visitors it was not likely to be discovered until Monday morning.

There was nothing for it but to keep moving, waiting for the radio to crackle into life as people discovered damage or missing articles as a result of drunken yobs finding their way home in the early hours.

After a very quiet first hour out and about, with nothing of particular interest to catch my attention, I was just making my way to the café when I was called to attend a report of a sudden death way up at the top end of town.

"Typical" I thought to myself "the others get to push paper and I get a body."

I had such a laid back approach to dealing with death that the operators always felt confident in calling upon me to attend, without the usual moans and groans. Because it was an early morning call it was more than likely someone expired in their sleep, not likely to be gory at all.

The worst case scenario was the ever so cruel event of a cot death, absolutely nobody liked dealing with those, and I prayed silently that it would not be the case.

I lengthened my stride as I knew I had at least a mile to cover, and although did not want to arrive out of breath, I wanted to arrive within a reasonable time of the call, as the relatives or person finding the body tended not to have clue what to do next.

Once again, although not the best job in the force, my desire to help others came to the fore. I could understand the feelings of the bereaved and tried to make the whole affair as easy as I possibly could.

As I arrived at the address I noted it was one of the large Victorian terraces, fortunately it was flat number one which tended to be on the ground floor. I used my torch to find the correct bell, the last thing I wanted to do was wake anyone else so early on a Sunday.

"Mrs Evans?" I asked as an elderly lady came to the outside door. I could see she was about eighty years old and had been crying, still holding a handkerchief to her face. She walked with the aid if a stick and slowly led the way to the flat entrance door.

"Oh yes, thank you for coming so quickly, you hear such appalling stories these days. It's my husband Fred y'know, he has really gone and done it this time!"

"What a strange statement" I thought to myself, but was sure there would be a follow up explanation forthcoming.

As soon as we stepped through the doorway I almost tripped over the body of a portly, elderly gentleman, fully clothed, lying prostrate in the hallway, half leant against the radiator. I quickly knelt down to check for signs of life but it was obvious from the discolouration on the underside of his face that he was long gone.

Mrs Evans had walked through to the immaculate living room and sat down on her favourite easy rise chair.

"I knew it, I just knew it" she wept. "He should never have gone out last night, it was far too cold."

"So do you fancy putting the kettle on and you can tell me what happened" I said gently. It was always a good idea to keep the living relative busy somehow to show a little bit of life carrying on as usual, even though their world had been shattered.

"I just need to know, has your husband seen his GP in the last two weeks that you know of?" I asked quickly.

"No, he's been as fit as a butchers' dog for years, you would never guess he was eighty two years old."

"OK, and have you called your doctor or anyone else apart from us" I probed.

"No, just you, I didn't know what else to do."

"That's fine, you make the tea, I just need to make some arrangements" I said as I stepped out into the hallway to use the radio to request a doctor to pronounce life extinct and arrange transport for the body down to the mortuary as a post mortem would be required.

"There goes my Monday morning off" I thought, still it was much needed overtime which supervision could not overrule so it wasn't going to be difficult.

"So, can you tell me what happened last night? How did he come to be in the hallway and why didn't you call us earlier?" I queried quietly and sensitively.

"Well, he went out to the local at his usual time. It was bitterly cold and I told him to stay in. As per usual he got a late lock in ("oops, didn't need to hear that" I thought.) I would usually expect him to be back by about twelve.

The doorbell went about one o'clock, it was Terry the taxi driver, nice man, he had Fred with him, but Fred was absolutely legless. He said he had found him lying on the path about two hundred yards away. Fancy him being on the pavement in this weather, silly old goat." She said with half a smile, pausing to catch her breath.

"God knows how long he'd been there. Anyway, Terry helped him to our door and then left. Well, I had just got the door closed when Fred just collapsed in a heap in the hallway. He is far too heavy for me to move, but he was fully dressed, still had his coat on. He was next to the radiator so I thought he would be OK."

"He started snoring so I left him to it. I went to bed, I remember waking up about four o'clock and went to the toilet, and he was still snoring away. Then, when I got up I thought it was quiet. I went to see to him, gave him a real good shake, but there was nothing, not a sound. He had rolled against the radiator, but I could see he wasn't breathing. That's when I realised he had gone" she sniffed again into her flowery handkerchief.

"Have you checked his pockets at all" I asked as I was worried that this may be a lot more sinister than first appeared, particularly as he had been found lying outside in the street, I had to rule out a mugging or worse.

"No, I would never go through his pockets," she said slightly offended.

"Just a minute, I need to check, you stay here."

A check through the pockets of the deceased caused, as I expected, a slight groan as I moved the body. The first time this had happened scared the life out of me, but I had become accustomed to it, as any remaining air in the lungs escaped if the body was moved and the body was not rigid with rigor mortis. To my relief I found his wallet, still containing cash, a pocket full of change, his watch and rings all present and correct.

I quickly removed the jewellery and checked for a necklace, it would be better for Mrs Evans to have the belongings now rather than increase the paper trail of security for his possessions. At least foul play could be ruled out. I would need to speak to the pub landlord to see how much he had drunk, to see whether he was paralytic or maybe hit his head in the fall. Either way the PM would reveal all.

The details required for the coroner's report were very specific and it was a credit to Mrs Evans that she could remember many of the required answers. I called her daughter and explained what had happened, requesting that she came as quickly as she could. Just then the doorbell rang.

I indicated to Mrs Evans to stay where she was as I could get there a lot quicker. To my relief it was a very tired doctor just finished a gruelling nightshift and on her way home. I explained the circumstances to her; the doctors made a quick check for obvious head injuries and tell tale blood from the ears but found nothing. She pronounced life extinct and signed the relevant form. It then meant that the body could be moved. As it was Sunday morning the body removers attended quickly and Fred's body was taken away.

I preferred to leave a grief stricken family alone, so I quietly completed my form filling and just as I was leaving her daughter arrived. I left them alone with their thoughts.

Right then, a quick trip to the mortuary to make sure continuity of identification was complete, the body correctly tagged and labelled, and I returned in time for my morning break. Normally anyone dealing with a sudden death was given a wide berth by the control room, time to sort things out, make follow up enquiries and generally deal with it as best they could.

As this one seemed straight forward and everything had been completed, I was asked to take over the area car for the south of the town as my colleague had got caught up in crime enquiries from the night before which would keep him busy for the rest of the shift.

It gave me chance to have a word with the landlord of the pub Fred had visited, and also make a phone call to a grumpy taxi driver Terry, who I had woken up after his late finish. When I explained what it was all about he was very apologetic and confirmed that the street had been very icy and he thought Fred had just slipped, being "well oiled" as he put it.

The morning passed uneventfully and there was just an hour to go before the end of the shift when I received a call to attend an address where there was concern for an elderly lady who had not turned up for church.

I arrived to find a group of people on the street outside the address. It was the first time in thirty years that Annie

Threadgold had not attended church and there were serious concerns for her wellbeing.

"Two in one day, what the hell did I do wrong" I muttered under my breath.

If this turned out to be another sudden death, then my finish at two o'clock would be in serious doubt. Being late home on a Sunday afternoon was tantamount to treason in our house, a definite time for the family to be together. Add to that the fact I would need to go in on the Monday, my rest day, and I could see the blue touch paper on a very loud bundle of fireworks being lit.

As soon as I enter our house, Angela could often smell the all pervading stench if I had been dealing with dead bodies and had learned over time not to hassle me, just give me a bit of space. I wasn't sure if that applied to Sundays!

I quickly established if anyone knew whether the occupant might have gone on holiday. Did she have any relatives nearby, or did any of the neighbours have a key? No positive responses to any of those. One particularly interested neighbour volunteered the information that he had tried looking through the windows but couldn't see anything, but the net curtains would not have helped.

"Right then" I said, "I need to find a way in which causes the least amount of damage and can be secured easily." Forget the scenes from the TV where the policeman kicks the door in with one lunge. A substantial door bolted from the inside, at the top of steps, is nearly impossible to kick in, and considerable damage would be caused. No matter whether the occupant was dead or alive or absent, there would still be the matter of making the premises secure again.

I looked around. As it was winter there were no windows open, and they all appeared to have good locks on. The doors were locked front and back. No response to repeated knocking and no reply to a ringing telephone from the control room. There was the old coal hole sliding cover but it was too small for me to get through. I then spotted a window which obviously led to the old cellar, it was already cracked. One of the few times I ever needed to draw my truncheon was whenever I needed to break in to premises in these circumstances.

The old window broke easily and I then decided to slip off my tunic to avoid any dirt or damage. Being midday I had not thought to bring a torch. I carefully slid into the darkness of the cellar, amazed that in this day and age it had not been converted like the rest of the street. It was indeed the old coal cellar. The air smelled damp and musty, and I could feel cobwebs everywhere.

My eyes grew slowly accustomed to the darkness as I waited. I could just make out the shape of the steps leading up to the kitchen, but as I moved towards them I stumbled on something and fell down. Cursing to myself I got up carefully and reached the steps, hoping against hope that the door at the top would be open.

Fumbling around for a while to work out which way the door would open, to my relief it opened inwards with a loud creak. I stepped into the kitchen and daylight, and realised with disgust that I was covered in coal dust, cobwebs and had a small cut on my arm, I had obviously nicked myself as I had crawled through the broken window.

"Hello Annie, can you hear me, are you there?" I shouted out.

From lots of previous experiences I knew the prime locations for the body may be the bottom of the stairs, the bathroom or the bedroom. I glanced quickly into the lounge and dining room but found nothing. I was calling out all the time, just in case Annie was around, but no reply.

I then noticed the landing light was on, something you could not see from outside. Maybe she was away on holiday and it was a security measure, or maybe not. Nothing on the stairs, I quickly looked in the bathroom and main bedroom, still nothing. By now I had resolved myself to the thought that Annie had gone away without telling anyone, so it was just as a last minute thought that I popped my head round the door of the smaller back bedroom.

What I saw gave me the fright of my life!

Not because of anything untoward, just that it was so unexpected. Sat bolt upright in bed, curlers in her hair under a hair net, wearing jam jar bottom glasses and a floral print nightgown was the person I presumed to be Annie!

"Annie, are you OK?" I said.

"What?" shouted the old lady, cupping a hand to her left ear?

"Are you OK, the neighbours were getting a bit worried?" I said in a slightly raised voice.

"What did you say?" she shouted. At the same time our eyes rested on the bedside table where I could see a hearing aid. Without having to say anything, Annie reached for it and put it in her ear.

"Now that's better, what did you say?" she said in a quieter voice.

I repeated my question, but could not understand how a strange man appearing in her bedroom in a locked house had not freaked her out.

"I've been calling and calling" I explained, "but you obviously couldn't hear me. You also didn't hear me breaking the cellar window to get in. I must say you don't seem too surprised."

"My Alfie used to be a bobby thirty years ago" she said, "I thought it was him, my eyesight isn't so good." Up to this point no mention had been made of Alfie or anyone else in the house.

As I queried that she said "oh no, he's been dead for 8 years now."

I saw my reflection in the mirror, black hands, cut arm what on earth must she be thinking?

"So how come you didn't go to church this morning?" I asked jovially, obviously relieved that I was no longer dealing with another sudden death.

"Well, I got out of bed at the usual time, but I felt awfully dizzy, so I daren't try going down the stairs, and I came back to bed. I just got lost in my book" Annie said in a voice which trailed off like a little schoolgirl who had run out of excuses.

"OK, how about you trying to get up now, I can help you if you want?"

"That would be nice." she smiled. She swung her legs off the edge on the bed, slipping into her slippers and rather unsteadily stood up. I passed her dressing gown and she put it on. She shuffled out onto the landing, with me standing by closely as she came to the top of the stairs.

"I feel OK now" she said, so I walked slowly down in front of her as she took one step at a time.

As we reached the bottom I asked her if it was OK to let her neighbours know she was alright.

"Of course" she said, "ask Maureen if she wants to come in for a cup of tea!"

Unlike so many times before in similar situations, I opened the front door to the assembled group, and with a big grin told Maureen that the kettle was on, and that Annie was safe and well, after having felt too dizzy to manage the stairs.

The inquisitive neighbour who had looked through the windows said "don't worry about that cellar window; I'll have it fixed this afternoon."

I popped back inside for a quick word with Annie and suggested that perhaps Maureen could have a key so if the same thing happened again there would not be all this drama. I declined the offer of a cuppa, it was nearly the end of the shift and I needed to get cleaned up.

"Wow" I sighed, "I thought I had seen it all up until now."

I radioed in to say all was in order and no further police action required. Now that is what they wanted to hear on a wonderful Sunday afternoon.

Chapter Ten

In the depths of winter the sleepy town was usually quiet, particularly when the weather was bad. When the wind was from the north it seemed to have a cutting action of its' own, a long nightshift seemed to last forever.

It was with these forlorn thoughts that I turned up for my standard nightshift, head bowed against the wind with tears running down my face but being blown backwards to drip off my ears, I was trying not to let my nose run at the same time.

I joined in the banter with the lads just going off shift and quickly caught up on station gossip, along with the usual greetings with the oncoming crew. You would think it would be a good idea to get a steaming hot cup of coffee or hot chocolate inside me, but I knew better! You just never knew when your next chance would be to go to the toilet, combined with the cold, the last thing I needed would be a full bladder early in the shift.

As the parade room filled up with the oncoming crew, it came as no great surprise to me that my allocated beat was to be in the town centre on foot patrol. Well, somebody had to do it. This was before the days where everyone had to go around in twos and wear body armour. I was known to be competent in handling myself in virtually any situation, and since my spectacular first arrest when I arrived in town the local lads knew not to mess with me.

Whatever respect it was possible to glean from the worst of society on the streets during a night time, I managed to do so. At least if they were local. I had spent a couple of years in the town and my face was well known.

That was all fine and well, but the cold wind was still blowing.

On nights like this there were a few tactics to get out of the weather. The first was an early arrest if there were any takers who wanted to push their luck, but that was not fair on the other lads if a fight kicked off in a town centre pub, as there were not that many available bodies when it came down to it.

Another was to arrange a meet with the van driver and jump in to try to get warm, some supervision turned a blind eye but others were known to frown. They had been there, done that, so that meant everyone else had to suffer. Plus, the visual presence of a uniformed officer still instilled a feeling of wellbeing in the more elderly drinkers and revellers out and about.

The cold wind usually got rid of the lingerers from the various congregation points outside the food outlets. Summertime there was no end to the chippies and burger places open for the visitors, but in winter it was down to the faithful two.

Ironically these places were ideal for the beat officers to go have a quick warm, but the owners were not too keen on having the uniformed officers so close at peak times, as they spoiled their street cred with the low life punters, who, after all, paid their ridiculous prices and kept them in business.

The only other rather sad way was to expect a call to a sudden death. Once again it meant an officer off the streets, but I would be warm!

Well, the job just had to be done. The bind was that you had to get dressed up like the Michelin man to protect you from the hours of cold, yet were expected to react quickly in any incident, and if that meant running, then so be it.

I drew my radio, then piled on the layers and made my short way into the town centre pedestrian area. Still in the style of traditional policing I was expected to rattle the door handles of every commercial property on my beat. If, in the morning, any premises had been burgled, the night duty officer needed to be able to state hand on heart that he had checked every one.

There was always a chance that supervision may venture out onto the street in the wee small hours when the town had quietened down, and suggest another "door check." Yes, it was traditional policing, but it worked.

I began the slow walk, taking note of the sights and sound around me and trying not to be too obvious what I was doing. It was remarkable just how many premises were left insecure. Often they would lock the door but forget to check the central bolts, so a slight push and the whole thing gave way. Other times they just blindly forgot to lock up, a mix up between staff. At other times the early burglars had made a visit. They had to be checked out, once again the cover your arse syndrome.

As the clock ticked and closing time came round, to the known flashpoint as the drinkers spilled out onto the street. Catch twenty two, the landlords knew the cops were keeping an eye on their time keeping, but it put everyone on the street at the same time. They didn't want to lose the last pint dash trade, but were expecting the look through the window from the passing bobby.

If the curtains were closed and a lot of noise was coming out of a pub, then a town centre "lock in" was frowned upon. It seemed to be accepted in the rural areas, but in town if one did it, they all wanted to do it. "Roll on the days of easier licensing laws" I thought.

As I expected, the drinkers came out onto the streets into the teeth of the northerly gale. Goodbyes were quickly shouted, never spoken, and they made their various ways home.

It was always necessary for available units to be close to the flashpoint areas, you would think it was an ideal time for me to have a chance to jump into the van for a warm up, but that cruel twist of fate, if I was in the van I was close to other police radios, and whenever anyone needed to speak there would be the wail of feedback giving away the obvious location.

Any officer who thought he would be clever and turn his radio off while he was with his mates only ever did it once. You could guarantee that an urgent call would come in, you all piled out to deal with it, and the one time, the only time, you need to shout for help on the radio there is no response. Why? Because you had clean forgot in the excitement to turn it back on! Plus your mate round the corner may be shouting for help on the radio, and you cannot be reached. Once bitten twice shy and only a fool would risk it. The standard answer radio black spot excuse failed to wash

Ironically, this was literally the time to stand around and get cold. Otherwise I could be off shaking door handles and keeping moving, or else trying to find the deepest recess in which to try to get out of the wind.

It did not take long for the weather to do the work an army of police could not. The scantily clad girls scurried off to the nightclub or got into waiting cabs, even their hardiness was being tested tonight. The town centre quickly quietened down with just a few minor incidents.

As there were no visitors around, the local antagonists didn't have any targets and quickly melted away.

"H'm" I thought, it is going to be a loooong night as I waved casually to the police vehicle drivers who pulled away to check further out of the town centre for mischief and accidents.

Trying not to look at the clock and wish the night away, I realised that I still had another two hours before my allocated break time, I just had to keep moving.

Just then the radio jumped into life requesting the traffic car to attend to a report of an accident on the coast road out of town, single vehicle off the road. "Probably a drink driver" I thought, with a little grin at the thought of the guys having to get out of their nice warm car in which they had been sitting for the past two hours.

A lot more radio activity took place relating to the accident, including a call for supervision and SOCO (scenes of crime officer) so it was obviously a very serious one and possibly either was, or could soon prove to be, fatal.

At the scene of an accident when it was very cold it was obviously worse if a casualty was trapped, or also if they went into shock, things could deteriorate quickly. I had heard the fire engine sirens turn out and head in that direction so knew things were not good.

The small town hospital was not geared to deal with major trauma, and any serious casualties had to be taken to the large city some twenty miles away. Not only that, because the area was rural, there were only ever two available ambulances for a large geographical area. One incident could tie them both up, leaving a vast area without a good response in case of other emergencies.

Saturday nights were not the time to require an ambulance, and the pathetic calls made by fallen drunk people often went unanswered, to the extent they got themselves home before the ambulance arrived. It led to a lot of bad feeling, but was all down to local politics and funding.

About thirty minutes after the call for the accident, I received a call asking me to attend an address just out of the town centre on one of the small housing estates. A teenage girl had been very seriously injured in the accident and had been taken to the hospital in the next town.

I was required to advise the parents accordingly. Other units were busy so it was necessary to pull me away from my immediate beat area.

I made a quick note of the name and address and headed off in their direction. It would be a good twenty minute walk uphill, so at least I knew I would get warmed up, but being the bearer of bad news did not warm the cockles of my heart.

As expected, when I arrived there the whole row of terraced houses were in darkness. If they had a doorbell that would be good, otherwise the "bobbies" knock would no doubt wake the neighbours on both sides, plus start off any local dogs barking in the night.

No sign of a doorbell, so a few short taps on the glass partition of the door to start with.

No response.

"OK, a little bit harder" I thought. Sure enough, a dog started barking next door, and an upstairs light came on at the house I wanted.

Just then the upstairs window flew open, and a heavy set balding man wearing a string vest stuck his head out and without looking to see who was knocking shouted out "What the fuck are you banging for at this time of night?"

"Mr Dougall?" I asked as quietly as I could.

"Oh, it's the law is it? What the hell do you want?"

"Could you come down to the door please Sir?" I asked in nothing more than a forced whisper, trying not to attract the neighbour's attention, which seemed a bit silly as the dog was doing a far better job than I was.

"What the hell can be so important that it couldn't wait 'til the morning?" he bellowed, making sure anybody who cared to listen got the full version.

"Please, just come down will you?" Something in the tone of my voice got through to the indignant Mr Dougall and he reluctantly muttered "just a minute."

Many people do not want police officers coming into their house, sometimes the smell of smoking pot, sometimes stolen goods clearly on view, and sometimes something as silly as a flashing traffic beacon drunkenly acquired on the way home, but they would be too drunk to work out how to turn it off.

I did not expect to be welcomed with open arms, but obviously needed to impart my message.

The hallway light came on and a dishevelled Mr Dougall appeared in his dressing gown. As the door opened I was greeted with the overpowering smell of stale alcohol on his breath which made me step back slightly.

"Don't stand with the bloody door open, it's freezing out there, come inside for god's sake man."

It may not have been delivered in the best possible tones, but it was a welcome invitation into the warmth where I had not had the chance to be for several hours.

"Well, what's so bloody urgent then" scowled Mr Dougall.

"It's concerning your daughter, Carol . . . ."

"Oh hell, what has she been caught doing now?" he huffed.

Suddenly a frail female voice came from the top of the stairs "What is it John, what's happened?"

"That's the wife" he said indicating quickly with a glance over his shoulder.

"I'm afraid there has been an accident" I said quietly.

"What was that John, what did he just say?" the voice became shrill and loud

"There's been an accident Martha"

"I knew it, I just knew it, it's Carol isn't it, is she alright?" shouted Martha Dougall.

"It is very serious I'm afraid, she has been taken through to Compton Hospital . . . ." I began to explain when there was a mild cry and suddenly the figure of Martha Dougall came crashing down the stairs in a flurry of arms, legs, dressing gown and nightie.

"Jesus" shouted John, "it's her heart, and it's very weak."

As I quickly checked over the very still, unconscious form of Martha Dougall my mind was racing ahead. This was a serious situation where I would need an ambulance, but I knew they were both tied up and probably twenty miles away at the moment.

There were no obvious cuts or broken bones which need attention, and she was breathing albeit very shallowly.

I anxiously asked Mr Dougall "can you get her medication so the hospital knows what she is on. She'll have to go to the local hospital in the first place, and I'll get some transport."

I called control and explained the situation, confirmed both ambulances were busy, so in a needs must basis I called for the police van, at least we could carry her in a laid down position. There was just not the available staff to come to attend to her, so any risk of moving her with any unknown injuries had to be tempered with the concern for her getting the correct treatment first.

I also asked regarding the condition of the injured girl. A short while later the response was that it was still critical but not looking good.

"What a decision" I thought as John Dougall returned with his wife's medication.

"We've got some transport on the way John, but you need to decide where you want to go. Martha will be in safe hands here, but Carol is in a bad way in Compton—where do you think you should go?" I asked delicately.

"God knows. I'd better go to Compton so when Martha comes round I can tell her what the score is with Carol." said John bewildered.

"You've obviously been drinking, is there someone who could take you?" asked I.

"I'll call Roger, my son; he would want to be there. I'll call him now" said John as the reflection of flashing blue lights bounced off the darkened living room windows as the police van came onto the street.

To any curious onlookers it must have seemed very unusual as three police officers were seen to carry a body carefully out to the van, just as Roger the son arrived in his car.

I had a quick word to confirm where he should be going and then we all left to take Martha to hospital in the town, John and Roger left for Compton hospital.

I quickly explained the situation to the concerned duty sister at the hospital and showed her the medication, gave as many details as I knew, and then asked a big favour.

"Could you possibly contact Compton for me and see how the injured daughter is doing?" I really needed to know. The sister quickly got through and after only a few sentences her face fell. She turned quickly to me and with a slight shake of her head she said quietly,

"She didn't make it; she died about twenty minutes ago."

"Oh hell," I thought, "I've sent the father and brother on a wild goose chase, they will be half way there by now". It angered me as I realised that when I had asked previously that somebody at that end had not known or had the guts to say she had died. And here was the wife and mother who, heaven permitting will come round, was without any family support and an horrendous shock to be told her daughter had died.

Suddenly I felt humbled in the knowledge that, tonight at least, my biggest worry was trying not to get too cold, and carry on shaking door handles.

Chapter Eleven

Have you ever walked out of a supermarket, or seen someone do the same, when the alarm goes off? The look on your face says it all! What me, no, not me, I haven't got anything, and then you blush more out of embarrassment than guilt.

All sorts of people resort to theft. The stereotypical image of a thief would be the masked man with the black and white hooped shirt depicted in the comics was so far from the truth it was laughable.

The more romantic term of shoplifting nevertheless was another way of describing theft. Why people would consider it any less an offence was beyond reason as far as I was concerned. When someone was convicted, the charge sheet did not say shoplifting, it was straight forward theft.

So why did people consider stealing from a shop any the less a crime than stealing a purse or wallet? It was only once they had been through the whole procedure of having been arrested, interviewed, charged and dealt with at court the seemingly innocent offence became a criminal record.

As I received the call to attend the local supermarket to deal with yet another shoplifter, I wondered who it would be this time. Maybe it would be a teenager being dared by his mates, a hard pressed young mum trying to make ends meet, or maybe a professional thief.

I made my way to the Managers office as usual where I saw the duty manager and the store detective standing by the desk. The only other person in the office was a white haired elderly lady, immaculately dressed, sporting several expensive looking rings on her wrinkled manicured hands. The quality of her clothes stood out and her recently styled hair and heavy expensive perfume gave off conflicting messages regarding her guilt or otherwise. On the seat beside her was a traditional wicker shopping basket, and in it was a small Yorkshire terrier.

The normal sequence of events was that the store detective would relate what she had seen. The manager would nod in agreement. Provided the events as related constituted an offence, it was then necessary for me to caution the offender, so that anything they said in way of explanation or defence could be repeated in court. This was mainly to catch out those who chopped and changed their story.

The store detective related how she had seen the elderly lady in the store. Rather than using a store wire shopping basket, she put her intended purchases into her wicker basket before going to the checkout. She also had the dog in the basket. She had originally been to the frozen meat section and then moved around the store.

The detective observed her going through the checkout, and although she had offloaded her purchases onto the checkout, the dog remained in the basket, somewhat excited.

She paid for what she had put on the belt from the basket and walked out of the store.

The detective then challenged the lady outside and asked her to come back into the store.

She was most indignant and proudly clutched her receipt.

In the privacy of the managers' office she was asked to empty her basket which she did. She was then asked to remove the dog which was sitting on a small blanket, and underneath there was a package of frozen meat which turned out to be a joint of beef.

This had not been put through the till. The fact that it was hidden under the dog and no attempt had been made to pay, showed intent to steal, and the act was completed as she left the store.

I cautioned the lady, speaking slowly and calmly to make sure that she understood what was happening. As I was well aware there would be numerous do gooders who would shout loud and long that it was unfair to treat an elderly lady in such a way.

As I questioned her it became apparent that she was fully aware of the situation. She did not offer any strange excuses, and when questioned to see if she had taken any medication that day she proudly stated that she did not need any. Little did she know that she had just blocked a frequent loophole alibi used by many other offenders.

Transport arrived and unfortunately for the lady she had to exit through the main doors into the waiting marked police vehicle. Only now did she appear to start showing any emotion, she was very much of the generation who placed great emphasis on whatever would the neighbours think. Would anyone recognise her?

I took pity on her and rather than subject her to a visit in the custody area, I decided to take it easy and go in through the front office. She would be treated as an NCV (non casual visitor) and placed in one of the interview rooms. It was as we got through the security door that the enormity of what she had done seemed to register. She became confused and then complained of feeling faint, then of feeling sick.

Fortunately a passing female secretary led her away into the toilet as I was left with the basket and a yappy little Yorkshire terrier. I found an empty interview room, left the dog and went off in search of a female officer to help with the interview, filling in the NCV book on the way.

Although the female officers were sometimes seen as uncaring and hard faced, they had seen it all and been tricked too many times to fall for any antics again. Even interviewing someone who could be their granny did not get them to drop their guard. I found Emma in the report writing room and turned on my charm, it should only take a short while.

The store detective had made her way up to the station and was writing out her statement. She caught me in the alleyway out of hearing of the elderly lady who had just returned to the interview room.

"This isn't the first time, y'know" she said. "I've suspected her a couple of times before but got distracted. This time I made sure I kept an eye on her, don't be fooled by the innocent little lady act."

I entered the interview with this knowledge fresh in my mind. The interview was short and sweet. As a parting shot, I asked,

"Have you ever done anything like this before? It is better to get it off your chest now before we find out. We get to check weeks of security camera tapes."

"Oh dear" she said. "Well yes, I take a piece of meat every week! The pension doesn't go too far and meat is so expensive these days."

Having checked records there was no trace of her having a previous record. I was certain that the prosecution department would not be taking any further action on this one.

Rather than charging her to appear at court, I informed her that the facts would be reported and she would be informed what action, if any, would be taken.

She shuffled out of the station taking the dog with her, but not the meat!

So, next time you see someone with the "I'm so innocent" look being escorted by store detectives, think on. Everything is not always what it seems!

Chapter Twelve

It was the beginning of the European shift pattern on a rainy Friday night as I rode my bicycle to work. That means three night shifts, quick change to two afternoon shifts and then another quick change to two morning shifts.

I found it was easy to get there as it was downhill most of the way and at the end of the shift I had a good mile of uphill slog to get rid of any pent up tensions on the way home before seeing the family or going to sleep.

Tonight it was working against me.

I had just had a blazing row with Angela over something and nothing, and now I was bringing my bad mood and problems to work, the first of three nightshifts from ten until six.

This was not good, not good at all. I needed to be calm and impartial, ready to deal with whatever came my way. I pedalled harder, even though I could free wheel most of the way.

Life in the job can become very serious so any light relief was always welcome. Just like most other walks of life, the proverbial wind up is a way of relieving the boredom, and in the police service there were no end of initiation rituals which were carried out on the never ending stream of unsuspecting probationer constables.

One of the biggest hurdles for them all to get over was the introduction to death. It is an everyday occurrence but the majority of people are sheltered from it, even in the case where an elderly relative dies they rarely get to see or touch the body except in some religions.

Now, I mentioned the unsuspecting probationer. Surely, with all the training college stories they must be aware that they will get a wind up; the only problem is they never really know if it is or it isn't until it shows itself for what it is. The subject is too sensitive to approach in a blasé fashion so laughter and merriment is not the ideal first approach.

I arrived the usual half hour early as I always liked to get settled in with plenty of time. I was in the locker room when one of the afternoon shift sergeants came in with a new face on the block.

"Hi Tom, how's tricks?" he asked, but without waiting for an answer carried on "this is P.C.917 Eddie Johnson, your new probationer."

I glanced quickly at the new arrival. He was very smartly turned out, slightly smaller than me but of stocky build and about 25 years old. His dark hair was cut very short in a square military style.

"Hi Eddie, Tom Springfield, welcome to the station, hang on a minute and I'll get you settled in." I said as I shook the hand of the newcomer, a surprisingly strong grip.

"Shit!" I thought. I had forgotten that I was to start with a new probationer, tonight of all nights. Eddie's reputation as a cocky know-it-all ex squaddie had preceded him. He had been put with me to round off a few rough corners and hopefully mould him into a good copper.

I slipped on my tunic, picked up my truncheon, handcuffs and helmet and closed my locker. I turned to give Eddie a once over on his uniform before roll call but, as an ex squaddie everything was immaculate.

"Oh, look at those boots!" I thought, noting how they had been buffed to a perfect shine in the way only the forces can.

"It won't take long before somebody scuffs those for you Eddie" I said as I looked down, "now don't get too upset when it happens!" I said with a fatherly grin.

I quickly checked that Eddie had all the right equipment, that his pocket book was prepared for the tour of duty with the correct times and date.

"Right, we now have to go draw our radios." I said as I led the way down the various corridors. As we walked into the sergeant's office I noted that my duty beat allocation was as an area car driver to the north of the town, and was just in time as the officer coming off duty was returning the car keys to the hook.

As I was showing Eddie the signing out procedure for the keys I heard my name shouted from the control room window. It was Shaun the afternoon shift control room officer waving a telex printout.

"Sudden death for you at the hospital!" he cheerily announced.

"Oh for Pete's sake, how thoroughly unoriginal" I thought. The off going shift had obviously got their heads together and decided a live body under a sheet in the mortuary would be an hilarious introduction for the new recruit.

"Bit daft for a Friday night shift," I thought, but decided to go along with it.

I briefly read the report, which I then passed to Eddie. A man's body had been brought in by ambulance after having fallen under the rear wheels of a double decker bus.

"Ha" I thought, "we don't have any double decker buses in town anymore, not that a newcomer would know the difference," but it made it all the more certain this was a wind up.

In the brief time I had spent with Eddie I realised sure enough he was a very over confident young man, cocky to the point of exasperation, it was going to get him into trouble at some point.

As I was already in a foul mood, I was not up to my usual standard of training performance. I had spoken briefly with Eddie who assured me he had seen action in the army and was not perturbed by the thought of dealing with dead bodies.

Now forget all the ideas you may get from the television that the forensic scientist is first at the scene and all the space age technology that comes with it. In cases like this the duty officer has to attend, strip the body, attach a label to the forehead and big toe, and then set about filling in all the details on a long form relating to the deceased.

We got permission from supervision to miss the parade briefing, showing them the telex printout, and were allowed to leave. Once out in the car park, a quick look round the vehicle for damage, tank was full, logbook filled in and all lights working, we were good to go.

As I drove through the light traffic, I would normally spend the time preparing the recruit for what he was about to see, smell and feel. I would let them know that it was OK to feel sick, to get out if they felt faint or at least say something.

But tonight my mind was still mulling over the argument with Angela. I reckoned that young Eddie would know all about those things, and so in a very remiss attitude did not prepare the ground before we arrived at the hospital.

As we arrived I noted another police car across the car park which I didn't recognise but didn't pay much attention to it. I thought maybe it was from one of the military bases nearby. As we walked in and strode straight through the casualty department we got a few cheery smiles and waves from the nurses, all the time I was thinking "yep, they are in on it as well."

We turned the corner and started walking down the long corridor; Eddie by now must have seen the only signs left—MORTUARY. I had noted that Eddie had a half grin on his face, he maybe guessed it was going to be a wind up but was going along with it. There was of course the chance that he felt totally ill at ease and was trying to cover up his feelings.

As I approached the doors, through the circular window I could see another police officer standing in the small glass cubicle office. I didn't recognise him, and as we walked through the door I spotted the officers helmet on the table.

"Oh Christ" I realised, "that is the helmet of the Petersfield Constabulary, the adjoining police force area." It suddenly became clear to me; this was not a wind up! The nearest town which had double decker busses was Cleardale in the Petersfield force area, but they didn't have a hospital, Denby had been the closest.

I introduced myself to the waiting officer who was obviously keen to get the relevant paperwork done and get home as he would be way over shift.

"He died in the ambulance on the way here, he's still on the stretcher round the corner, but is a hell of a mess I'm afraid" he said as I signed the required paperwork and got the details I required. With that the officer from Petersfield was gone.

"Bollocks" I thought, "I have got this so wrong." I turned to Eddie who still had the half grin on his face; he had obviously not noted the strange force helmet.

"C'mon" said Eddie in his cocky fashion, "let's get this over."

"I guess you think this is a wind up don't you?" I asked in a quiet and delicate tone.

"Of course it is" replied Eddie with a smirk.

"I'm really sorry Eddie; I thought it was that's why I didn't prepare you. I reckoned you had been there, seen it all and wouldn't need any preparation."

"What, you mean it really is a dead body, sudden death investigation?" Eddie said, his eyes going wider by the minute and his face becoming paler.

"We don't have double decker buses, so I thought it was a story. BUT, Cleardale does, even though it's out of our force area we have the nearest hospital. Didn't you notice that officer was from the Petersfield force? Right, as you say, let's get this out of the way."

I showed him the paperwork which had been prepared and pointed out the various "must do" actions required.

We left our helmets and tunics in the office, donned plastic aprons and rubber gloves and walked around the corner to where the body lay on the stretcher.

"What a sight!" I thought to myself, one of the worst I had seen. I glanced sideways towards Eddie, but could see his pale face was now as white as a sheet, beads of perspiration showing on his forehead.

"If you are going to be sick or faint, the sink is over there and you can sit down." I said quickly just as Eddies hand flew up to his face and he raced across the room, retching as he did so.

"Hmm, maybe not so battle hardened as he would have us believe" I thought, although the sight before us was rather gruesome.

The corpse was laid on its back, half curled with the legs at an horrendous angle and trousers soaked in blood. One arm was obviously broken and sticking out at an alarming angle, and there was drying blood which had oozed from his mouth.

The body was too fresh for the familiar nostril pervading smell of death, but there was a mixed smell of stale alcohol, urine and body contents.

I walked over to the quivering Eddie who was looking a slightly better colour and very sheepish.

"Sorry son, I thought you would have seen worse than that where you've been."

"You don't get a lot of that in the stores" replied Eddie. So, it was all bravado then. I could see that as a major breakthrough in getting past his obnoxious cockiness.

At least he had not met the rest of the shift yet, so as first impressions count we could head off a major problem.

"When you are ready we have to strip the body to look for signs of identification. Everything is recorded so you can write and I'll do the poking around. All possessions go into one of those bags and we seal it with a special seal. Get a good lungful of the smell, the sooner you get used to it the better." I instructed.

"Look, he must have been pissed, his eyes are glazed" I quipped. This was an effort at humour, one of the ways experienced officers learned to deal with dead bodies, the alternative was to collapse inside with all the compassion and reverence associated with death but it made it impossible to handle.

Most officers and undertakers have a wicked sense of humour in these circumstances, but never let it show when relatives are in the vicinity. The moisture on the victims wide open eyes had begun to dry out and given a cracked eggshell glazed effect.

As I stripped the body I realised getting the trousers off was going to be a problem, so I cut them off in two halves. As I removed them and the underwear, I made the gory discovery that the man had been carrying a tin containing tobacco for rolling his own cigarettes.

The crushing action of the bus wheels had squashed the can, splitting the corner which had acted like a knife; the pressure had pushed the can in his pocket deep into his groin. It has sliced clean through the scrotal sack and through the femoral artery at the top of his leg.

His innards and testicles had then been squeezed out into his underpants.

I guessed that the ambulance staff had realised with the massive loss of blood and that his vital signs would have been so poor there was not a lot they could have done for him.

As I searched through the pockets, apart from a few coins, and the baccy tin, there were no clues as to his identity. I checked the small pocket high in the waist band to discover a tightly folded piece of paper. To my amazement when I opened it there was a telephone number, one that I recognised. It was that of our local police station, and the extension number was for CID.

"I think this guy is a CID snout" I observed to Eddie who was struggling to keep up with events.

We finished stripping the body, labelled it head and toe, and removed it from the cutting table to the large storage fridge, ready for the post mortem the following day. I had to explain to Eddie that our shift was going to be changed, because of continuity we would need to be there for the post mortem. The possessions were packed away; we stripped off the gloves and aprons, put them in the bin and went to the office. It was now getting late and all available personnel would be required in town, but I needed duty CID to come down to the mortuary to help with identification.

I made the call and then suggested we went for a coffee to the nurse's station. Eddie nearly threw up at the idea, so I thought better of it and decided on a breath of fresh air instead.

A short while later the two duty CID officers arrived, introductions were made and I told them about the piece of paper. The body was covered with a sheet so was not such a shocking sight, and as they saw his face one of them said "It's Gary. Gary Benson. God knows where he's living now, bit of a homeless sort. You could start with George Willis, if anyone would know he will."

"You've really drawn the short straw tonight" I sighed as I turned to Eddie. "George is one of the town lowlife alcoholics. He hates the police, lives on the roughest estate. Still. It's good to know you are getting a baptism of fire."

Usually the alcoholics tended to be off the streets before it got late. The damage had already been done and they were drunk, skint, and a possible target for gangs of yobs out on the town at night.

We finished the relevant paperwork, had a quick chat with the duty nightshift manager in casualty, and made our way out to the car. Now I had to get my early warning act together, otherwise Eddie might just get himself in a spot of bother.

"Where we are going is a real shit hole. We have to park the car where we can see it at all times. Do not accept any offer of a drink, it will either have some unknown substance in it or they will spit or piss in it. Don't sit down, if the kids are about don't touch them, and don't tell them your first name. Got it?

"OK." grinned Eddie.

This was going to be fun. George was no stranger to having a police car outside, was more than used to having the house searched by warrant, and often arrested forcefully for whatever misdemeanour he had committed. His wife was a very large tattooed woman who nobody, but nobody, ever wanted to tangle with.

It was just after midnight when we pulled up outside. The front garden looked like a scrap yard and obstacle course all rolled into one. There was a light on upstairs so hopefully they were still up. As I knocked on the door the downstairs light came on and a figure appeared behind the grimy front room curtains.

"It's the filth" a voice was heard to shout from inside. Heaven knows what activity then occurred. If it had been a raid the back door would have been covered, so in this case if anyone did go out, they were not seen.

"What do you want?" George shouted through the letterbox. Even from there I could smell the stale alcohol. God what a life.

"I need a word George, you've done nothing wrong."

"Huh, I've heard that before. I'm not opening the bloody door so sod off" he growled.

"I need to ask you about Gary Benson, where's he living now?" I said quietly.

"Sod off, I'm not a bleedin' grass" was the reply.

"Look George, there has been a serious accident; I think it might be Gary and I need to speak to his next of kin." I said calmly but firmly.

"Well, it can't be him. I was drinking with him in Cleardale this afternoon and he wasn't coming back, so go annoy some bugger else" snapped George.

"Was he wearing a blue polo neck jumper and grey trousers" I asked.

"Well, yes, I think he might have been, how do you know?"

"'Cos that is the same as the person I have who was run over in Cleardale earlier tonight."

"Just a minute." said George.

It took a long while of coming and going before I heard the bolts on the door coming off, and then the huge frame of Connie Willis filled the door.

"What's this about Gary?"

I was shocked. Normally her voice was hard as steel, but now it had an edge of concern and tenderness which I had never heard before. She was obviously not as worse for wear through drink. I quickly explained the circumstances and said I needed to inform next of kin.

"I've known him twenty years" she said "I'm probably the closest thing he's got. We have some of his gear here."

"In that case, I know it's a lot to ask, but could you come and identify him for me please. If I'm wrong, I'm sorry, but we need to know. I will take you down and run you back."

"OK, give me chance to get dressed. Do you want to come in?" she asked.

"No thanks, we'll wait outside" I said, avoiding the risk of everything mentioned before.

She quickly appeared and squeezed her frame into the police car, her rank body odour instantly filling the small space. At least it was only a quick hop to the hospital.

When we got there, I sent Eddie off with instructions to go find the coffee machine as I prepared a quick statement for Connie to sign. I knew from previous experience that it was necessary to get as many details as possible as soon as possible. Once the person sees the body they often go to pieces and you cannot get a lot of sense out of them.

I had never seen the more feminine caring side of Connie before, and suddenly realised that, yes, these lowlife scum were human beings after all.

Eddie returned with the drinks and the paperwork details were completed as far as possible. The statement was prepared quickly and then it was time to show Connie the body. People react differently every time, so I did not know what to expect, but had the box of tissues at the ready. I hoped to goodness that she didn't faint as she was so big!

She gasped as the sheet was drawn back, her eyes filled with tears and she turned away, it was indeed the body of Gary Benson.

I quickly ushered her out, back to the waiting hot sweet cup of coffee. She signed the witness statement and looked at me through bleary eyes.

"Jesus, you guys have got some rotten jobs haven't you?"

"If only you knew the half of it, and that people like you make it a lot worse" I thought bitterly to myself.

"We do what has to be done" I said in a gentle way. I became aware how both sides now saw each other in a different light, but guessed that the next time I encountered her she would be the snarling monster as always.

We ran her home, returned to the station, by now Eddie had recovered his appetite, had our break and I showed Eddie how to fill in the various forms before going off shift early to be back in time for the post mortem.

"Welcome to the world of front line policing" I said to Eddie," you have had a hell of a start, it can only get better!"

As tradition required it, we turned up in uniform at the hospital mortuary at 10.00am the following morning.

It had only recently started that autopsies were being carried out on Saturdays, but it was an attempt to balance the workload. Because we were supposed to be on night shift, if it didn't take too long we could chalk it up as overtime and resume the nightshift pattern.

If not we would be allocated different shift duties.

Angela swore blind I had purposely changed my shift to avoid her and lumber her with the weekly shopping run without my assistance. To show preference attending a post mortem rather than being with the family was a particularly sickening scenario, yet no amount of explanation would placate her. I couldn't promise to be back by a certain time and this was before the days of late night opening.

I was pleased to see activity in the mortuary as we arrived, meaning hopefully we would not have a long wait.

"Morning Tom" came the cheery greeting from the mortuary assistant Frank Cooper "I see we have a student" he smiled, shaking Eddies' hand as I introduced them to each other.

"Seeing as you are here I guess you get first pick" he grinned, "the boss won't be long".

As if on some hidden command the swing doors opened and the massive shape of Bill Evans filled the space. He was a dour faced mammoth of a man, a bit of a bully to his staff yet purportedly very good at his job. He was known to be meticulous in his work and never took anything for granted.

Yet again introductions were made and as soon as Eddie and I had got our gowns on Bill was ready to start.

"Now young man" he boomed at Eddie, "take some really good deep breaths after the first cuts start, fill your lungs and KEEP breathing. If you try to hold your breath you will collapse!"

He quickly commenced the incision to open up the chest cavity as Frank produced a large pair of cutting pliers to open the ribcage. I looked sideways at Eddie, perspiration on his brow but features hidden behind a paper mask.

"Breathe Eddie" I said quietly, having observed no apparent movement in the mask.

The post mortem rapidly moved on, checking the lungs, the heart, liver and kidneys for weight and condition.

"Do you smoke young man?" asked Bill to Eddie.

"Only socially" was the very quiet reply.

"Well, just you look here" pointed Bill as he expertly sliced open the left lung. "That is what happens if you smoke" he lectured as he pointed out the black, tar like substance in the bottom of the lung and general condition. "That area should be pink!" he spluttered with indignation.

"Each to their own" I thought, wondering what the insides of this enormous man wielding the scalpel would reveal.

Bill muttered to himself as he inspected the heart, then as he opened the liver he shook his head in amazement.

"This guy was walking dead!" he exclaimed, "How on earth can a liver like that function properly?"

"A lifetime of daily abuse and tolerance" I said.

"Well, we wouldn't need to pickle it if we wanted to save it now would we?" quipped Frank with a grin showing in his eyes behind his mask.

A quick inspection of the damaged stomach, a few pokes and prods around the damaged area and then a quick inspection of the brain which Frank had deftly exposed and the job was almost done. The next bit always amazed me.

I saw Frank pick up a copy of "The Sun" newspaper and walk towards the cutting table. I looked over to Eddie who was still trying to comprehend the proceedings.

"It's not coffee break yet Eddie" I said teasingly. I watched as Frank collected the various body parts which had been removed from the chest cavity. He replaced them very casually in their approximate locations, then picked up the newspaper and inserted it into the space on top of the organs, effectively covering them.

He then produced a pre-prepared length of stitching line with needle and quickly sewed up the open wound, "the newspaper holds all the bits in while I stitch" he helpfully explained to a wide eyed Eddie.

Well, he had made it through without puking or fainting, the job was over within an hour, so we made our way back to the station, finished the paperwork and went our separate ways before returning in the evening.

At least I might be out of the doghouse with Angela and get the shopping done!

Chapter Thirteen

"Have a guess Tom!" called out Duty Inspector John Clegg as he was allocating the beat duty for the forthcoming Saturday night shift. It came as no surprise to me that I had been put on foot patrol in the town centre, especially now as I had young Eddie Johnson, my new probationer, in tow.

Part of being a tutor constable to a probationer was that before doing or saying anything, it was necessary to hold back and see what the probationary constable perceived to be the best course of action. Obviously in times of great urgency there was not the luxury of this protocol, but at all other times it was necessary to count to ten before taking any action, and if possible discuss what the best course of action would be.

In their wisdom, the powers that be did not recognise the power of discretion when considering a probationer. Everything was considered black and white, and the public were often in for a big surprise when faced with a raw recruit. They had to learn the ropes, to handle people and be prepared to enforce the law when required.

It was always easier to deal with minor cases first, to get them used to the paperwork and build confidence, all the time letting them know that after training they would get free rein to apply discretion, common sense or just good policing when dealing with the public. Although they would only be under the wing of the tutor for ten weeks, everything that they submitted to the prosecutions processing department had to be squeaky clean and clear cut.

Many times, as a tutor, it was necessary to stand back and let them dig a hole and see how they were going to extricate themselves. To see a drunken yob drop fish and chip papers and ask him to pick it up was a classic test, see how they could handle the situation which could, and often did, escalate out of control.

I had given Eddie a copy of the town centre map the night before, and as a sort of homework had asked him to learn the main streets. Often people would ask directions and it was part and parcel of the job to be able to give them, plus if a chase ensued and you caught a suspect after a few streets, you needed to know where you were if you needed help. This was where the quiet hours of the early morning came in useful, learning the shortest routes and locations of the major landmarks.

As Eddie and I signed for our radios, I noted that the rain had started again. It was pointless to get soaked to the skin early on, as you just did not know what was in store, so it was a case of taking up a position in the town centre in a wide open doorway, sheltered from the rain but still in full view of the people trying to enjoy their night out.

It is assumed that the probationer is familiar with the basic definitions of the laws of the land; god knows they are drummed in verbatim at training school. Others can be learned as they gain experience. It was always a testy situation if it became apparent that the probationer knew some law had been broken, but not which one, and worst still, whether there was a power of arrest attached.

"Nights like tonight ought to be cancelled" I muttered as we both stared out onto the empty streets, an occasional group of drinkers moved between the pubs or clubs, but nobody was hanging around in the relentless pouring rain.

"At least it will be a quiet night" piped up Eddie with his youthful exuberance.

"Maybe so, but you will soon learn quiet nights, rain and cold do not bode well. After you have looked at the town hall clock for the tenth time and sworn it had stopped, you'll realise. C'mon, let's go find some business!" I said as I pulled my collar up a bit higher against the cold and wet.

I believed that I held the station record of having been out on the beat eight minutes before I had locked someone up on a rainy night, and was back in the dry. The offender had just smashed a large plate glass window after a row with his girlfriend just as I had come around the corner.

Let's see what tonight might bring.

It did not take long for us to come onto the main drag in town, part of the town's one way system, and surprise surprise, coming towards us in the wrong direction without lights was a family estate car. I nudged Eddie to get out there and stop it.

Eddie snapped into action like a little toy soldier and literally marched out into the middle of the road with a perfect police stop hand sign. The car stopped dead in the middle of the road. It was then that I saw a distraught female driver in her mid thirties, the windows steaming up and what appeared to be four teenage kids in the car. As she wound down the window you could see she was at the end of her tether, uptight and tearful.

"Could you pull over to the side of the road please?" asked Eddie in his best authoritative tone.

She duly pulled over, fortunately there was very little traffic and no serious risk was being posed.

"Do you realise you don't have your lights on and this is a one way street and you're going the wrong way?" asked Eddie in his clipped military style.

"I'm so sorry" whimpered the woman. "We've been to the pictures but the car wouldn't start. We waited ages for the breakdown man who got us going, and he told me the fastest way to the bypass would be down this way. The kids are fighting, I'm cold and wet and totally lost!"

"Just a minute" I said as I led Eddie to one side. If ever there was a situation where things would go from bad to worse this was it. To try to fill out his first fixed penalty ticket in this weather would be silly, and he would totally alienate the young mum in the process.

"She obviously knows she has done wrong but it appears to be a genuine mistake. There is no suggestion of her having been drinking, so I would suggest you give her a docket to produce her driving documents if she hasn't got them with her, I'll do a computer check for you."

As Eddie returned to the car he could see the woman shuffling through a bunch of papers.

"Here are my details" she said "handing them out through the half opened window." I hoped Eddie knew what to look for as he received the results of the computer check. Eddie looked up and nodded, it appeared to agree with the paperwork he was reading.

"Everything seems OK" said Eddie, "just remember your tax will be out at the end of the month."

"Well spotted" I thought to myself, even I hadn't clocked that one.

"When we get you turned round and you have your lights on, follow the road round to your right and turn right at the end, you will see the signs for the bypass from there.

If you just wait for this car to go past, we'll stop anything coming as you turn round. Take care!"

"Oh my goodness, thank you so much" she managed a weary smile as she turned on the lights and closed the window.

"So, how do you think that went?" I asked.

"I can see what you mean about the ticket, but she broke the law so I would have given her one."

"Sometimes you just need to see the bigger picture. I'm not saying we let everyone off, just judge each incident on its' merits." I said conscious that the lad was keen to do his job, and the tendency to apply discretion had softened me up a bit.

We were now beginning to get very wet; I could feel the dampness on my shoulders.

"We need to get out of this rain, so we either shiver in a doorway or find a customer for the nick" I said.

As we came to the square I could see the burger van in its' usual place. It sells burgers and kebabs; the quality of which was below basic, but the drunken revellers seemed to eat anything. Personally my stomach lurched if I got a whiff of the hot fat and "cooking" smells.

The van was positioned to catch people coming from the station, just past the pedestrian crossing after the zig zag no parking zone. It was a classic place to catch illegal parkers, a three point instant penalty, even though there was ample parking close by.

The number of people who thought that if it was raining it was OK to park there. They would put on their hazard warning flashers (the 'park anywhere lights') and go off to get some food.

Well, the whole idea was for safety, and when it was cold dark and rainy, I considered that would be even more important for the area to be kept clear.

"Just give it time" I said to Eddie "it's like fishing!"

Sure enough, after several minutes a flash sporty saloon pulled up right behind the van and parked on the zig zag lines. It was being driven by what appeared to be a vivacious young business woman with red hair who sure enough switched on all four "park anywhere" indicators.

She stayed in the driver's seat as three other giggling beauties got out of the passenger side "and don't forget the curry sauce" we heard the driver shout just before they closed the door.

Just as Eddie had puffed out his chest, took a deep breath and started to cross the road, we both gasped as we saw the driver reach down into the passenger foot well and then saw her take a drink from a two litre bottle of something.

"H'mm, maybe more than meets the eye here" I thought.

As Eddie tapped on the driver side window the young woman jumped a mile, she obviously had not seen us coming. As she opened the window a cloud of cigarette smoke billowed out, mixed with the overpowering smell of some expensive perfume.

"Have you broken down?" Eddie asked.

"No, nothing like that, we are just getting some food" she said, flashing a wonderful perfect glistening white smile. Just then a whoop and giggle came from her friends as they saw that she had attracted attention from the law.

"Then can you tell me why you are parked on these white lines?" he asked flatly.

"Oh c'mon mate, we're just getting some food." She smiled sweetly.

"It's an offence to park here without due cause, so I'm afraid you have earned the right to a fixed penalty ticket. Is this your car?"

"Well, it's a company car really. Can I just move it over there?" she asked pointing to the nearby parking spot she should have gone to in the first place.

"It doesn't work like that. Now, have you had a drink tonight?" he queried, he thought he could smell a trace of alcohol on her breath but the perfume was very strong.

"Just a couple of cocktails" she said innocently.

"And can you tell me what is in that bottle in the foot well then?" he asked, indicating with a knowing look to her left hand side.

Her eyes rolled to the top of her head in a desperate sign of despair.

"Let me see . . . ." he asked as she reached down and slowly brought up a half empty two litre bottle of cider.

"Can you turn off your engine please" he said.

Eddie had just done a vehicle check and the results came through for an out of town advertising agency.

Sometimes there were insurance problems when vehicles such as this were not being used on business.

Eddie had been getting ready to issue the fixed penalty notice, but I motioned for him to put it away.

"She has been drinking, difficult to say how much, but she needs a test. Request one of the traffic boys to come here with a breath test kit. We will have to wait a few more minutes anyway as she has been smoking, and we just saw her take a drink so the alcohol in her mouth needs to clear."

I knew we had to be careful here. We had just seen her take a drink from the bottle, and she would need a full ten minutes for the alcohol to clear from her mouth so that a false reading would not be obtained.

I primed Eddie on last minute reminder for the breath test. Eddie then went to speak to the driver to tell her that she would need to provide a breath sample, and asked the routine questions to make sure she could provide.

The traffic car took a while to arrive, and without getting out in the rain, they passed out the kit to Eddie. I could see his hands shaking as he put the sample tube onto the device, checked the indicators and administered the test. As he pressed the sample button, the amount of time it took for the indicator to change was a rough idea of how intoxicated the driver would be. Green light changed to amber, red amber, a painful few more seconds and then red.

"Jackpot" I thought, Eddie was going to make his first arrest. As Eddie informed her of her rights and cautioned her, the stunning young lady stepped out of her car to show she had a drop dead gorgeous model figure, as she struggled to put on her coat. The traffic guys couldn't get out of their car fast enough!

As she was led to their car, I approached her three friends, by now silent and shivering under the overhang of the burger van.

"Is any one of you entitled to drive this car that hasn't been drinking and is fit to drive?" I asked, not expecting any takers. "In that case if you want to get your coats and belongings, we're taking it in."

They quickly got their bits, I motioned for Eddie to escort his prisoner in the traffic car and I slid into the driving seat of the sports car. A quick familiarisation with the controls and I followed the traffic car to the station.

When we had got settled into the bridewell area, I had already briefed the custody sergeant that it was Eddie's first arrest and to be patient as he led him through the official breath test procedure, covering his back for any oversights which may occur. After all, it was the sergeants' responsibility.

In the bright lights of the cell area it quickly became apparent that the female driver was a naturally very attractive person. Although she wore make up it was not overdone, and she certainly knew how to flirt with the lads! I had mentioned to Eddie that because of the slight delay in the reading registering a red, she may prove to be a borderline reading, but it would be decided by the reading from the machine.

A female officer arrived to check the prisoner, and the paperwork was just getting completed to get the second test underway when all hell let loose as the van arrived with three violent drunken yobs. For her own safety she was moved to an interview room for the time being.

"This is not good" I explained to Eddie. "The longer it takes to complete the procedure the more chance there will be that she will scrape through".

The last thing I had expected was for Eddie to tell her that! She obviously had him under her spell, and was trying to delay things as long as possible. I asked to speak to Eddie outside.

"Be careful, your judgement is getting clouded. You aren't going to get a date out of it so don't be drawn in!" I said. "Just because she is fluttering her eyelids doesn't mean you stand a chance, she would eat you for breakfast. Worse still if you did get involved she would expect some preferential treatment."

Eventually we were called back in and she increased the flirting level with the custody sergeant. He had had a rough night so far and was certainly not in the mood for her antics. When she stuck out a pet lip in mock sadness, I could just see the film cameras rolling.

She didn't even try hard to provide the first sample required. When the sergeant explained that if she didn't try harder, in his opinion he would put down that she failed to provide, and that was as bad as a fail. The second time she tried harder and managed to meet the required readings on the alcometer computer.

The printout coughed into action, and as expected her readings were just over the limit. When it was explained to her that she had an option of providing a urine or blood sample for further more definitive analysis, she jumped at the chance. Arrangements were made and a urine sample taken. That meant she would have to wait for laboratory analysis, and would not be charged until the result was known.

Eddie was so keen to get her released that I had to quietly remind him why she had been questioned in the first place. He needed to report her for the offence of parking on the hazard warning lines, and also needed to check all the vehicle paperwork details, so once again the paper trail continued

As she was still considered unfit to drive she would have to make her way home and pick up the vehicle in the morning. Her little girl pouts when requesting a lift home fell on deaf ears.

It had fallen well, just in time for the meal break as she was escorted to the front door.

At least it had stopped raining outside, mission accomplished yet again!

Chapter Fourteen

The parade briefing was short and sweet, not a lot to take in. An interesting vehicle out for observation was a minibus stolen from an adjacent town, which was believed to have been taken by a group of children in care. For whatever reason the seaside seemed to attract runaways and it was considered that it may come our way.

Eddie Johnson, my probationer constable, and I had already reviewed our paperwork prior to the briefing, there was little we could do during the nightshift and we were quickly out onto the town beat.

Duty sergeant Colin Shepherd did not like anyone hanging around after the briefing and expected us all to be on our allocated beat as soon as possible. So saying, it was an absolute no no to hitch a lift with an area car or the van to get to your area unless it was an emergency.

Being a midweek summer evening the area was quiet, a good time for me to show Eddie all the various nooks and crannies worth knowing. Local knowledge was critical if you wanted to stay one step ahead of the customers, whether it was short cuts to get to a place in a hurry, dead ends to finish a chase or just being able to direct strangers to the nearest toilet/shop/bank etc.

It was also a time to show a visible presence and have a game of I-Spy with the local characters and villains. Because the money was all gone and giro day was a couple of days away, the frequently loud and noisy ones were often subdued, content to hang around various locations.

This often annoyed some traders who did not want them being there, but I knew only too well that the yobs at least knew a few of their rights. Provided they weren't obstructing the walkways or causing other anti social offences, any attempt to move them on was met with hostility and even if they condescended to move, they would return shortly afterwards.

I always used their reluctance to move as a positive thing. I would chat to them, playing up to their bravado and see who could justify their street cred amongst their mates.

Little did they know that in trying to outdo each other in bragging rights, they often dropped vital pieces of information which could be the last piece of a jigsaw to a non related incident.

Keeping a mental note of who was wearing what clothing was vital. In an area where money was tight, some young yobs would wear the same top for months. They thought it cool, I called it a godsend.

Whenever an incident had occurred involving the local youth, descriptions given by witnesses were generally vague, but always related to a top or a hat being worn. To know who usually wore that top was imperative, because whenever a group activity occurred they would temporarily swap tops to confuse the police.

It was always good fun playing them off against each other regarding tattoos'. If one of them had a new one, they were often proud to show it off. With ego boosting comments like "I bet that hurt" or "wow, that's distinctive" I found that I could get them all comparing their artwork.

My memory was accurate, and as soon as I had a quiet moment I would jot down everything I had gleaned to be passed on to the LIO (local intelligence officer.) What the numbskulls didn't realise was that in hot weather when they were out in T shirts and tank tops, or even in cold weather when they strip down in a drunken rage during fight scenarios, they were just flashing distinctive beacons to witnesses.

Many people do not remember faces, but could almost always describe a tattoo, its colour and location on the body, a perfect opener in the search for a perpetrator.

If I let them know I was not in any rush to move on, then after a while their street cred began to diminish if they were seen talking to the filth, even worse they could be accused of being a grass. It soon worked when they became uncomfortable and decided they needed to be somewhere else.

As the group were starting to leave another youth turned up on a BMX bike several sizes too small for him. He kept his distance from me but there was something just not right about him. I had not seen him or the clothes before, but definitely something familiar about him.

His hat was pulled way down trying to hide his face, but dangling down there were long curly ringlets of hair for want of a better term, but the hair colour was an unnatural reddish brown.

The youth shot me one last glance as he rode off which is when I spotted them! Two tell tale teardrops tattooed on his cheek. From what I remembered, those were the old style self inflicted borstal spots which had been enhanced to look like tears.

I radioed in to control, was there a report of Jimmy Lewis having escaped again?

Jimmy Lewis was a one man crime wave who had finally been remanded in the high security young offenders unit many miles away. He had managed to escape twice before, and always returned to his home town.

He had been brought up by a Mum and Dad who were in fact his grandparents. The person he thought was his older sister was his Mum. When he found out at the tender age of twelve he totally rebelled, stealing from anyone and everyone, family, friends, neighbours and strangers.

He was not normally a violent person; he preferred opportunist and sneaky theft.

"741—We've checked with the unit, he hasn't escaped." Pete Knowles in the control room responded a few minutes later.

"Strange" I thought. I made a note of the clothes the lad had been wearing, along with the hair and the teardrop tattoos. I then discussed the various members of the group with Eddie, giving him the rundown on everything I knew about each one. Some of them were only a couple of years younger than Eddie but had quite a different lifestyle.

Darkness was drawing in and the streets became quieter, even the holiday makers were taking it easy. A slight on shore breeze brought a chill to the air and I was glad I was wearing the regulation black leather gloves to keep warm, even on a summers' night.

We had done our routine round of door handle shaking to confirm that all premises were secure and had settled into the doorway of the council offices. It had a large entrance with a couple of steps. A perfect vantage point to watch traffic and pedestrians, we were in full view to be seen if required, but the recess just took the wind off us a bit.

Standing there was more habit than necessity in summertime, but it was a definite advantage in winter.

Eddie was learning to just stand and observe, absorbing the information he would require in the future.

"Quick, there it is!" I yelled as I ran out into the middle of the road.

What Eddie had failed to see was a minibus approaching the small roundabout to our left and coming straight towards us. I suddenly remembered the observations request from the briefing but could not recall the index number, but there was no mistake even in the streetlights that there was a young driver and several young passengers.

As I indicated for the minibus to stop it suddenly swerved round me and took off. I was on the radio in an instant and reported that the minibus had gone the wrong way up Church Street, to alert other patrols which may have been in the area.

Eddie could not believe his eyes as he saw me race off up Church Street like a dog chasing a rabbit. Church Street was a steep one way uphill winding street, with traffic flow downhill. There was a tall wall without pavement on the right, and shop fronts with a small path to the left. No parking places, no turning places.

"470—Assistance on Church Street please" came over the radio. As luck would have it, detective sergeant Carl Peters just happened to be on Church Street in the unmarked CID car. It was not a matter of setting up a road block, one car coming down the one way system literally blocked the road.

What I had observed was that the young driver had set off, but as he swung into Church Street he would not be expecting the steep uphill gradient round the corner. He was not an experienced driver and struggled to find the right gear to manage the incline and nearly stalled the vehicle, giving me chance to get close.

That panicked the young driver even more who then bunny hopped up the road probably in third gear. It was just one of those marvellous things that Carl had been coming down Church Street at the right time.

I arrived puffing and panting as Carl was standing by the drivers' door of the minibus.

The group of youngsters, all apparently fourteen or fifteen years old, did not seem to have any fight left in them. They were in a strange town, hungry and tired and just wanted to go home, they had had their fun.

As there was no room to turn, I decided it would be easier for Carl to reverse back up to the top junction than try to reverse the minibus down the winding hill. Fortunately only one other car had arrived behind Carl and they agreed to reverse as well.

I was about to get into the minibus when a red faced and breathless Eddie joined us. Initially he had not even bothered to start running up hill, he couldn't see the point trying to chase a moving vehicle. It was only when he heard Carl on the radio that he realised the minibus had been stopped.

"Jump in" I shouted as I got in to drive the minibus. Eddie had not got his breath back as he climbed in with the group of runaways and looked very sheepish.

The minibus was taken back to the station where the kids were all given a hot drink. There were no food facilities open and, generous to a fault, I did not feel like sharing my sandwiches with anyone!

Arrangements were made with the care home to pick up the minibus complete with kids and they were asked to bring something for them to eat.

I was ribbed by the others about chasing cars, after all my nickname was "Terrier."

Eddie was ribbed at being outrun by someone nearly twice his age.

The rest of the shift passed without incident, an hour of paperwork time was granted and we made the most of it.

As I arrived for the following nightshift, there was an unusual buzz in the station.

During the previous night there had been a spate of burglaries up on one of the housing estates.

Add to that the young offenders unit had issued a countrywide telex reporting the escape of one—Jimmy Lewis. It turned out that during the morning headcount his absence had been noticed.

"Crikey" I thought, "he must have been out during the afternoon to get back to town by yesterday evening, what sort of lock up were they operating?"

The description given in the telex was totally wrong compared to what I had seen the day before. He had obviously dyed his hair or was wearing a wig. Fortunately I could give the entire shift an accurate description, including clothes and hat for them to look out for.

Young Eddie was not on shift tonight as he was due away on a course in the morning, so I was by myself on foot. CID would be out and about on the estates, their car had changed since Jimmy was last put away and he may not recognise them until too late.

It would be a waste of time having a uniform presence in the estate area, as he would be off like a shot.

Often there are a string of coincidences which lead to a good result in policing.

WPC Kath Montgomery had reason to call on a house on the estate near to where Jimmy's 'parents' lived on a non associated matter. She completed her paperwork in the kitchen, but spotted three teenage lads in the front room as she passed. What she thought was unusual was that even though they were inside, one of them was wearing a hat pulled down over his face. Although it had been dimly lit in there, she was sure it had been Jimmy, according to my description given earlier.

Because of the nature of the address, there was no way she was going to attempt a confrontation by herself.

She drove a safe distance away and radioed her findings. As I had seen him the night before it was decided that I would be picked up from the town centre by Tommy McFarlane in the area car and meet up there on the estate.

CID did not want to blow any cover they may have by turning up at that time just in case she had been mistaken.

It was decided that Kath would make the arrest with me as back up. Tommy would stop outside with the police cars.

Kath knocked on the house door once again with me standing to one side. As the door was opened by the woman she had been talking to previously, a figure suddenly rushed from the back of the kitchen up the stairs. I was certain it had been Jimmy and pushed past Kath as she explained to the resident what was happening. Jimmy had obviously seen the two cars outside and knew he'd been rumbled.

I took the stairs two at a time and saw the figure go into the back bedroom. As I ran into the room it came as no great surprise to see the window wide open. It was one hell of a jump but I guessed Jimmy would be away down the drainpipe.

Kath had remained by the door as I shouted to her to get outside round the back, but by the time I got down there I could see Kath at the bottom of what could jokingly be called a garden. It led on to a series of allotments. I shouted to her to bring the car round and head him off as I shoved my helmet towards her as that was one thing I could do without.

It was beginning to get dark and I didn't rate my chances of catching him as he took off in a series of hedge hops. I ran along the back and could make out the high chain link fence of the tennis courts ahead. "Aha" I thought "got him!"

To my dismay I saw the lithe figure of Jimmy climbing the chain link fence like a monkey. There were a couple just finishing their game on the tennis court and the man quickly realised what was happening. As Jimmy swung over the top and was ready to drop down the man shouted "I've got him."

He held his arms out to catch Jimmy and what happened next was farcical. Jimmy landed in front of him, slipped through his arms, ducked down and crawled between his legs before running off towards the exit.

With a groan I radioed progress to the other units and ran round the edge of the tennis court. The noise of a police car being driven at speed came from the far end of the tennis club car park. It was enough to warn Jimmy who ran off down the alleyway leading to the play area which backed onto fields.

He had cleverly run away from any vehicular access so it was down to me. What was annoying was that when these youngsters were banged up, to keep them occupied they used to run keep fit exercises to burn off excessive testosterone. It just meant that when they were released (or escaped) they were mega fit. The way he went over the fence, it was no surprise that he had escaped detention.

I saw him run straight for the wall at the back of the playing area, he leaped over it in one jump and disappeared. My approach was a little more cautious as I looked over the wall to see quite a drop. Jimmy was just scrambling to get up but was now running with a limp. I quickly found another way round and continued the chase. Thankfully it was downhill towards the stream at the bottom of the grass field some three hundred yards away.

If he kept running across the field I reckoned he would continue up the other side and come out somewhere near Four Acres farm house on Stubble Lane. I radioed for Tommy to head him off up there.

Jimmy climbed over a barbed wire fence, waded through the stream and started off up the field of barley on the other side. I was tiring and did not fancy the uphill slog. I struggled over the fence, ever conscious of the paperwork if I were to damage my police property uniform, got across safely and started the uphill chase, young Jimmy still keeping up a good pace, limping all the while.

Just then I saw the headlights of a vehicle pull into the gateway at the top of the hill. An over eager Tommy had pulled the police car into a gap. Jimmy was caught in the headlights as dusk was falling quickly.

He realised he was running into a trap so turned and ran sideways. It gave me a chance to close the gap as Jimmy turned back towards the housing estate. I was now only a hundred yards behind. A thought crossed my mind:

"Would he really be so stupid to run to his 'parents' house?" I puffed the idea into my radio and Kath acknowledged.

Sure enough he ran towards the estate, thankfully I could see a small bridge across the stream this time. As he got back to the estate he ran home, an address known to all the officers. Kath was just getting out of the car as Jimmy ran through the back door of the house. With a final burst of speed I had closed quickly and literally crashed through the door after Jimmy.

"Watch the windows" I shouted.

I ran up the stairs past the astounded 'Mum and Dad' who had come into the hallway, guessing they had seen all this before.

I saw the front bedroom door closing as I got to the top of the stairs. High on adrenaline I would not be stopped and charged at the door. It flew open to reveal Jimmy brandishing a knife in the corner. I was far beyond reasoning and negotiating. I quickly grabbed hold of the single wardrobe next to him and pulled it forwards, causing Jimmy to drop the knife and protect himself from the falling wardrobe and its' contents.

It was enough to give me the chance to pounce and use probably more force than required to get him handcuffed before yanking him out from underneath the fallen wardrobe. Just then Tommy appeared at the door realising that he would not be required.

I told Tommy to have a quick look around the room for possible articles stolen in the previous night's burglary spree, as I led the now subdued Jimmy out to the waiting police car I saw the supervision car pull up with Inspector Tony Donaldson just getting out.

"Well done Tom. Blimey, look at the state of you, you need to get fit!"

I suddenly became aware that I was obviously red faced, breathless and sweating. I noticed ruefully that my quarry young Jimmy, now sitting in the back of the patrol car, had hardly broken into a sweat.

So, a two mile chase through allotments and fields carrying full police gear, doc martin boots and threatened with a knife, against a youth in trainers built like a racing snake. The Inspector has seen none of it.

"No contest!" I thought, wondering just what sort of operation was needed to become an Inspector, so out of touch with life on the street it was unreal.

Chapter Fifteen

I arrived for my ten 'til six day shift full of the joys of spring. It was a bind having to work a weekend day shift, particularly with the kids at home. An early turn finish at two in the afternoon would have given me the rest of the day with the family, or a night shift even, but the day shift only came round once in a while.

It was a cool cloudless Saturday, a slight mist burned off the river early and it had the makings of a wonderful spring day.

In itself that was great, but with it came the realisation that the small seaside market town would become filled with day trippers causing all the usual hassle with traffic, parking and associated matters.

As always, as I was starting "mid shift" there was not the usual parade turnout with the rest of the shift, I just needed to check in with the duty sergeant, find out my allocated beat duty and then start the day. It came as no great surprise that I would be on town centre foot patrol, after all, that was the main reason for the dayshift on a weekend to show a uniform presence on the streets.

It also gave a little bit of a chance of catching up on enquiries and paperwork checks in the area, as people were more likely to be home at the weekend. Although not able to carry a large paperwork folder around with me, it did give me chance to come face to face with people and arrange a more suitable time to deal with whatever the matter was about.

There was an unwritten rule that if you had been allocated a foot beat that it was bad form to still be in the police station at the beginning of the shift without good reason. A quick check of paperwork and messages showed me where my priorities lay, then I was off out into the town centre.

The traffic was just beginning to build up as people fought over parking spaces actually in the town, rather than having to park on the extremities and walk in. The locals become frustrated if "their" parking spots had been taken.

The god given right assumed by many to be able to park outside their own house on a public road frequently gave rise to heated disputes. Strange cones and objects appeared in several places to reserve their places, heaven forbid if some legally minded stranger had put two and two together and realised the objects had no legal right and meant they could park there.

Strange how tyres suddenly became flat or scratches appeared on the offending car with nobody in the area having a clue as to how it could possible happen!

It never happened when the locals parked there—how unusual?

All the small eating houses and stalls were just about open now, even though the numbers on the street were still relatively low. As always there were the odd few street traders peddling their wares. They knew the score and the legit ones were always quick to produce their peddlers' certificate when requested, the others squirmed and wriggled at the sight of a uniform, quite amusing really.

As I made my way down to the busier riverside walk my attention was drawn to the sound of loud music in the distance. There were no particular places I might expect to hear such a noise in the area, and as I made my way towards the sound my radio sparked into life.

"We have a complaint of noisy buskers opposite The Emerald Shores restaurant" was the quick message from the civilian operator in the control room.

"Yep, I'm just about there" I acknowledged, "I'll soon have it sorted."

The "noise" was that of a loud electric guitar being played reasonably well, and some garbled singing vaguely resembling a song of some sort. I drew nearer to the restaurant, a posh place with a very good regional reputation and always well frequented, not the sort of place one would associate with this noise.

I then realised that the "buskers" were in fact on the opposite side of the street, using the high walls of a warehouse building to reflect their "music," but then became aware that next to them on the pavement were a fair sized amplifier and a couple of car batteries! No wonder they were managing to produce such a racket.

Normally people passing by a busker either throw a few pennies in the hat, or pretend they are not even there. These two were having the effect of driving people to the other side of the road!

Given the time of day, the younger generation were not in great abundance, and the more elderly visitors to this normally quiet part of town would expect to tolerate a light folk type music rather than heavy rock at this time on a Saturday morning.

I was surprised when I approached the two buskers. I would normally expect a somewhat downbeat unkempt appearance, appealing to the people ready to give to the down and needy. Not these two!

The one holding the guitar was wearing a good quality shirt with brightly coloured tie, with a waist coat and matching trousers and shiny black shoes. The other holding a microphone was dressed as a teddy bear!

Upon my arrival the cacophony stopped abruptly, raising an impromptu round of applause from the passersby, more because the long arm of the law had arrived than to show appreciation of their murderous rendition of a timeless classic.

I was met with a beaming smile from the guitarist and a friendly wave from the bear.

"Is there a problem officer?" enquired the grinning guitarist, "We are just trying to raise some cash for this charity" he said, pointing to the rather small sign on the pavement.

I was immediately somewhat taken aback by the very well spoken voice and demeanour of the guitarist, not your usual street musician.

"There could be" I said, "We've received a complaint. I'm not sure if it is about your musical abilities or the volume." I continued in a light hearted way.

I glanced down at the equipment. It was very sophisticated for a street performance, and by no means in keeping with using the natural acoustics of the area.

"What made you set up here?" I asked quizzically.

"The Emerald Shores is always packed with people with lots of money in their pocket, so we thought it would be a good catchment area" said the well spoken guitarist.

"I can see the reasoning behind that, but on the flip side do you really think that it would be their type of music?" I queried?

"H'm maybe not, but we can play all sorts" he volunteered eagerly.

"I think it is the volume as well, I could hear you from the High Street"

"Wow, cool!" responded the bear in muffled tones.

"Right Guys first of all let's have some details and let me see your street performers licence please" I said, triggering just the response I expected.

A quick worried glance went from the guitarist to the bear, unknown returned glance from the bear.

"But we are collecting for charity, didn't know we needed a licence" said the now flustered guitarist.

As I explained the finer points of busking in a small market town, the byelaws and regulations had just about any street activity covered. They might get away with it in the larger towns which didn't have the time or inclination to enforce these laws, this one did!

With the best intentions this couple who were from out of town had fallen foul of the law! I requested personal details of the two, and as I asked the guitarist his occupation, I was astounded to hear the reply,

"I'm an air traffic controller."

He must have seen the surprise in my eyes and then grinned widely.

"If you're surprised at that, wait 'til you ask him." He smiled, pointing to the bear.

I motioned for the person in the bear to remove the head piece. As he did so it revealed a fairly plump very red faced man in his mid 40's with a somewhat sheepish grin.

"So Sir, what could be more intriguing than a street busker being an air traffic controller?" I joked, not quite sure what reply to expect.

"I'm a so . . . . ahem . . . a solicitor!" spluttered the now exposed bear.

"A solicitor" I mocked, adding to the man's discomfort. "But you didn't know it was an offence to perform without a licence?"

"No, No, I deal in conveyancing property and family matters" he replied somewhat embarrassed.

"Well, I can see your actions were admirable but you have gone about this the wrong way. Even with a licence, playing at that volume in this location would not be acceptable."

"Where would be acceptable then, if we had a licence?" asked the guitarist.

"Good question, how about the big car park out of town" I joked, not really wanting to give them any future hope of being able to perform.

After a bit of banter the couple agreed to pack up. And not only move on but move out.

I realised that to take any form of legal action against the two, who after all were doing things for the right reasons, would be counterproductive to community policing and I let them go with a few words of advice.

"Problem solved, no further action" I radioed, feeling a cuppa coming on at my favourite tea spot further up the road.

The town began to fill up and I continued on my beat, more like a walking tourist information bureau, but that was the nature of the job.

Lunch break would be about one thirty p.m and so I would have chance to meet up with my regular shift starting at two o'clock as they came on duty. As I got back to the station it suddenly became apparent that today was Grand National day, I had nearly missed out on the sweepstake organised by the control room staff.

As it happened there were a few straggling outsiders still not claimed so I put a couple of quid on them, knowing that anything could happen in that wonderful race. I wasn't normally a gambling man but half the prize pot went to charity anyway.

The shift briefing came and went, and just then I heard my name being called down the corridor. There was a confused elderly lady who had been brought to the front desk and my help was needed. It appeared that she thought she had walked the forty miles or so from her home town and just didn't have the energy to walk back!

Many times before similar things happened to elderly people who arrived by coach on a day trip, then somehow become detached from the more mentally coherent in the group.

A quick check of her handbag contents revealed a bingo card with her name on, issued in a town about sixty miles away called Sandholme. She couldn't recall having been on a coach, but didn't have any rail or bus tickets in her bag, yet still insisted that she had walked all the way.

As Robin Needham, the area car driver was still in the building, I arranged a lift for myself and the elderly lady up to the coach park but was daunted to find about forty coaches all parked up. As the lady remained in the patrol car, I quickly walked along the back of the row of coaches, scanning the company names and town of origin advertised on the rear of the coaches.

Jackpot! "Jameson Luxury Coaches, Sandholme" jumped out at me in gold and red lettering on a white background.

I went to the front but there was no sign of the driver. The coach was too high up to look inside, but what normally happened if a driver had to kill time, he would probably go to the nearest café for a breakfast /lunch then get his head down, often on the back seat.

I pulled my truncheon out to act as an extended knocker, and tapped on the side window next to the back seat. Nothing! I tried again a little harder, then again a lot harder.

Just then a sleepy eyed head appeared, saw it was a copper in uniform, and motioned that he would come to the front.

"Do you recognise the old lady in the police car?" I asked.

The driver couldn't say for sure as they all looked alike to him, but he did know that even though they were here on a day trip, they had all been planning to go to a brass band concert at a place called "The Coliseum" sometime in the afternoon.

I thanked him, apologised for the disturbance and jumped back into the car. We both knew the location and were there in a few minutes. We were just getting out of the car when a very worried official looking man in tweeds approached us.

"I'm terribly sorry officers, but we seem to have lost one of our party." He gushed, oblivious to the fact that the officers may have other things to do.

"Would you care to look in the back of our car sir?" I grinned, hoping against hope that we had the aforementioned missing party member.

"Mabel, where have you been?" he exclaimed as he saw her sitting there, "thank goodness you're alright!"

Mabel was helped out of the back of the car into the waiting arms of a now growing group of concerned elderly people. She simply could not understand how some of her friends had also walked all that way on the same day. How would they ever get home?

Robin and I left her in their capable hands, and, oh, look at the time, good reason to return to the station in time for the race!

The shift sergeant was turning a blind eye to the handful of officers hanging around the building waiting for the start of the race. After all, it was only once a year. As the runners were coming onto the course an incoming call sounded on the switchboard.

"Tom, there's urgent call from Mayworths' department store, two young shoplifters have just done a runner." Jenny shouted from the switchboard.

"What a bit of bad timing!" I cursed. There was no way I could delay until after the race, it was my beat and duty called. I had previously had a good relationship with the store detective and didn't want to spoil that.

I quickly made my way into the town centre and arrived at the main entrance to be greeted by the store detective in an agitated state.

"I nearly had 'em but they did a runner" she proudly announced, not only to me but anyone else in earshot. "They got away with half a dozen cassette tapes I think."

"Do you have a description?" I asked, knowing it would be good and detailed.

"There were two teenage lads about fourteen years old. Both my height, slim build, one with short straight sandy hair, freckles, yellow v neck jumper and black jeans, the other had long collar length dark curly hair wearing a black imitation leather jacket and blue jeans."

"Great" I thought, "good description, but still like looking for a needle in a haystack."

I didn't give away my thoughts as I thanked the store detective and finished making my notes, passing the descriptions to control to pass out to other patrols.

It occurred to me that I had missed the race!

"By the way, who won the race?" I asked as an afterthought.

"Dunno but it wasn't mine!" came the disillusioned reply from the store detective.

"Oh well" I thought, "Maybe I'll have better luck finding those two lads."

The town was now thronging with locals and day trippers alike; it was good to see the hustle and bustle all around. Even though I had a good description of the two juvenile shoplifters, I felt it would be really difficult to spot them in the crowds.

As I was walking slowly down the riverside, I paid particular attention to the crowded amusement arcades where the teenagers may be drawn. There were hundreds of them, how on earth would I find them?

True to form, my positive thinking or "coppers' nous" was going to be my salvation.

At exactly the same time as I saw them, they saw me. It seemed like my brain was running through syrup as I slowly registered—blond hair black jacket, dark curly hair yellow v neck jumper—they had swapped tops! Even that slow recognition was not required, as they both suddenly split apart and ran in opposite directions, confirming in my mind they were the two I was after.

The blond haired lad made a dash up the nearest side street he could find. All I had to do was walk briskly over to the entrance, comfortable in the knowledge that the side street was in fact a dead end yard blocked in by a huge overhanging cliff.

"He would need to be a mountain goat to escape this one" I thought as I radioed for Robin in the area car to come to my location.

I entered the yard but there was no sign of the youth!

"Well, he has to be here" I thought as I started to look around, "unless he lives in one of the cottages."

"Police dog is going to be released, show yourself now" I bluffed as I shouted the warning.

To my amazement I heard a scuffling sound, and then saw a pair of feet and black jeans emerging backwards from an old disused dog kennel half way up the yard!

Sheepishly the teenager stood up, brushing off dog hairs in the process.

"Where are they?" I asked.

"Where are what?" countered the youth innocently.

"You had something in your hands when you ran off. I haven't seen anything so I would guess it is in the kennel. Now get it out or else!" I barked at the nervous youth.

The instant response by the teenager made me realise that I was not dealing with a streetwise kid, so this might not be such a difficult case after all. The lad quickly ducked back into the kennel and came out with a handful of cassette tapes, still wrapped in cellophane.

As I cautioned and arrested him on suspicion of theft I heard Robin on my radio asking for my exact location. The car quickly arrived and the youth was unceremoniously placed in the rear of the estate car. We officers knew from previous experience that things may change quickly, so the lad was handcuffed to the anti roll handle above the window behind the passenger seat.

Because I now knew the other youths' description had changed, I passed it out to other patrols with the latest sighting. I knew the lad would have melted into the merging crowds, but would show up somewhere. I pressed the arrested youth to find out how they had travelled to the town. It appeared that they were in a minibus party stopping overnight at the local youth hostel.

"Well if all else failed, I bet he'll turn up there sometime" I said to Robin.

"We'll just have a look round the area" I said, my instincts still on edge.

Sure enough, we had only travelled a few hundred yards when I spotted a flash of yellow amongst the crowd, the tell tale dark curly hair on top. As I jumped out of the car the youth spotted me and ran off.

It was not safe to chase him in the car due to the high volume of pedestrians in the precinct, so I raced after him, thankful that I did not have bulky winter clothing on.

I caught sight of the youth running down the riverside, water on one side and crowded shops on the other. As the youth was struggling to get through the crowds I was closing quickly following his cleared route. He would soon run out of places to go as the river mouth was ahead leading to the beach.

It dawned on me that the pace had now steadied with a constant space between us. I was not quite fast enough but the youth was running out of steam! Tenacity was always one of my strong points, and my ability at cross country running would come in to play.

Once the youth was on the beach he really didn't have anywhere to go. I couldn't see the point of calling for the dog section. I radioed for Robin to drive to the far end of the headland, and so between us it would only be a matter of time.

I was reluctant to chase him onto the beach knowing the salt in the water and the sand was going to play havoc with my shiny polished boots! Still, there was no alternative but to follow him.

As I ran onto the beach the youth ran up to the water's edge where the sand was firmer and easier to run on. It was pointless running towards the piers, so he chose to run the other way, towards the headland as I had guessed.

I continued to run after the youth, acutely aware that I was only maintaining the distance and not closing on him.

A few hundred yards ahead of the youth, I could see a man walking two large Rottweiler dogs on leads, close to the water's edge. With the little amount of spare breath left in my lungs I managed to shout;

"Police—stop him!"

The youth was sandwiched between the man with the dogs and me. He had the option of running into the water or across the loose sand on the beach. The man with the dogs bent down and let the dogs off their leashes. The dogs immediately ran towards the youth who stopped dead in his tracks.

They continued to run straight at him, getting there just before I did. It was obvious to me that the youth was scared of them, but a quick observation showed that the little stumps where a tail should have been were wiggling in playful delight.

The owner was desperately calling them back, and as both myself and the youth had stopped running there was no longer any fun in this game, so they ran back to him.

I breathlessly grabbed the equally breathless youth and arrested him, cautioning him as best I could. I realised I didn't have my handcuffs which were on the other youth in the car.

There was no fight left in the youth and I hoped he would come quietly. The dog owner had re-leashed the dogs and came up to the breathless pair, all smiles.

"They're not vicious, just playful, a bit of a handful" he guffawed.

"Great to hear" I panted, "thanks very much."

I radioed for Robin to come to meet us at the nearest access. As I looked over towards the youth I could see that this one was a bit more streetwise and was probably the leader of the two. I decided to strike while the iron was hot, and the youth knew no better.

"Your mate gave us the tapes, now you have to tell me where you have hidden the other stuff." I told the surprised youth.

"What other stuff?" he tried to answer.

"Don't try kidding me son; I've been in this game too long. If you don't tell me we will come and search the youth hostel and the minibus" I growled, very confident that if the lad thought his mate had told me all that already he may have told me some more.

It was a gamble that paid off, but I didn't quite anticipate the answer that came.

"There is a lot more under my mattress at the hostel!" He said quietly.

"Oh my gawd" I thought "this is going to be a right can of worms."

The car arrived and only then did the youth see his mate was still in the back.

Even he could work out that there had been only a little time to talk to the other youth, he had been tricked!

Both were warned not to speak to each other and we all four drove back to the station in silence. I had radioed ahead and asked the store detective to attend the station to make a statement of complaint on behalf of the store, including full descriptions and a reference to what goods had been stolen.

Because of their ages the two would need a responsible adult with them when being questioned. It turned out they were on a minibus trip visiting several towns during the week, a trip organised for under privileged children by their local church group, and wait for it, one of the accompanying responsible adults was a serving copper!!!

As the two were processed and kept in separate secure rooms, I borrowed the keys for a spare car and made my way to the youth hostel. A brief enquiry as to the small group quickly established that two of the carers were present, indeed one of them being the policeman.

"How embarrassing this must be" I said with empathy.

"Comes with the territory" said the somewhat shocked officer through gritted teeth.

"Can you show me which bed Tony Thornton uses please" I asked, knowing I had the effective guardian of the youth with me.

On lifting the mattress a gasp of surprise came from both the carers. Hidden underneath were three pairs of jeans, two tops and assorted small items, some with labels still on.

"I think we can assume these are all stolen" I said, "I need to take them with me. Just for good measure, where does Steve Cross, the blond haired one sleep?" I queried.

"I think it was this one" pointed the other carer. As I lifted the corner another treasure trove of stolen goodies was revealed.

"Oh dear, looks like the kids have been having a rare old time" I said, noticing that some of the labels were from well known stores not located in this town.

"I hate to mention this, but better to say it now than find out later, is there any chance any of the other lads will be actively stealing as well?"

Both carers looked at each other, and I saw them both take a sharp intake of breath as the policeman carer reached to another mattress three beds away. Oops, another haul.

"No, No, No" I thought, only a couple of hours of the shift left and this was becoming a massive "roll up" as it was known, where a simple single investigation was to reveal numerous other crimes and defendants.

I called control requesting to meet with the duty CID officer, who, I was informed, was out of town on enquiries.

"Damn it!" I cursed.

As the other bed occupants were not present or in custody, several protocols needed to be observed. I agreed with the policeman carer for him to await the return of the other members of the group, tell them the game was up and to come clean. I would return to the station with the other carer to commence the interviews and would await a call when the others had returned.

A cheer went up as I entered the back doors of the police station.

"The story of the roll up couldn't have got out and was nothing to cheer about anyway, so what was all that about?" I wondered.

"Congratulations Tom, lucky beggar" said Pete coming out of the control room, handing me an envelope, "Your share of the winnings!"

Only then did I remember that it had been Grand National day, but I couldn't even remember the name of my horse.

"It came in first at forty to one" said Pete, "so you get the lions' share of the sweepstake."

"Hee hee, I was probably the only one who didn't watch the race" I thought.

The carer must have wondered just what a den of iniquity this police station must be!

Just then I caught sight of detective sergeant Carl Peters coming in through the back door, I knew he was just coming on for a split shift nights duty so would not be tied up right now.

I quickly explained what I had got, how I thought it may roll up to five or six defendants with untold thefts. Although the range of the theft may appear petty, it quickly became apparent to the sergeant that numerous single crimes could be detected and written off, always a good thing for the crime figures.

Although he told me he would allocate the oncoming detective constable to the case, he would not take over the investigation so it would be a joint effort. A quick check with duty sergeant Colin Shepherd that it was OK to incur overtime, another call to my long suffering wife to say I would not be home until late, and I set to with the necessary paperwork and interviews.

The problem with thefts of this kind is that the perpetrators never really pay any attention to the shops they steal from. Unless there is a recognisable brand label and store locator on the item it is often impossible to get a statement of complaint to prove the offence.

As it happened the jeans still had labels on, for a well known store in the next town of Cleardale. I confirmed with the carer that they had indeed been there the day before.

"Cavalry is here!" I heard as the happy smiling face of Trev Cartwright, the oncoming duty detective constable, appeared round the door.

I quickly tried to explain all the circumstances.

"You should have stayed in and watched the race!" Trev quipped jokingly.

Fortunately for me, Trev had been brought up in Cleardale, still had family there and knew the shops in the area very well. If the youths could describe roughly where they had been, Trev could take a guess at which shops some of the stolen gear had come from.

The two lads were now getting hungry, scared and fed up, so they were eager to offer any help they could to speed up their departure.

Just then the custody area phone rang. It was a message for me. A P.C. Grainger was at the front counter asking for me. This was the other carer.

The entry glass to the front access door was frosted, but it did not disguise the fact that there were several people standing in the entrance lobby. As I hit the security switch and swung the door open my heart hit my boots. Not only was PC Grainger there, but he was accompanied by another adult and FIVE more youths, all carrying black bin liners with what I must assume were more ill gotten gains.

My "roll up" had just got bigger!

As each youth was processed the list just got longer and longer. All the stolen gear had to be bagged and tagged, keeping track of just who had admitted stealing what and from where. The evening dragged on into the night.

It was impossible to determine who could be charged with what until the owners of the property could be traced. As it was Saturday night then this would more than likely mean enquiries on Monday, and many of those would need to be passed to other forces. I was thankful to have CID involved as their inter force departmental co-operation was a bit more co-ordinated than uniformed branch.

Slowly but surely the youths were reported for their individual crimes and bailed to return if required to face further charges. As PC Grainger led the last one out, he told me that the trip had been called off and the entire group, including those not suspected of anything, would be returning home that night.

As I surveyed the scene in the report writing room I ruefully shook my head.

The original two had been caught red handed. Because of the difficulty of finding the owners of the property, those thefts could have been TIC'd (taken into consideration.)

It was because of the involvement of the rest of the group that the "roll up" of recordable and detectable crimes became so great that it would appear to be a feather in our cap for the crime detection figures. Life was not just straight policing, office politics often got in the way.

As an operational street bobby, I had done the initial location and detection. It would now be up to the CID and file preparation unit to gather the bits of paper required and for me to piece them all together into the finished case file.

Upon initial review, seven defendants with eighty nine pieces of stolen goods between them would be a great notch in the detection figures.

The infuriating thing for me was the knowledge that the time and effort that this case would take to bring to juvenile court would, no doubt, be wasted with a smack on the back of their hands and a warning not to do it again by the do gooder panel. "They are tomorrows' criminals in training." I thought.

As Trev and I decided it was time to call it a day and for me to go home, I glanced at the clock.

"Oh my gawd" I grimaced, "nearly ten o'clock on a Saturday night."

There would be no use appealing for reason as I returned home to Angela.

The kids would all be in bed, she would be fuming and I was tired out.

"Aha" I thought as I felt the envelope in my shirt pocket when I put on my civvies jacket, "maybe those winnings, along with the overtime, might give me a reprieve!"

Chapter Sixteen

"Can you come over here with me please, my Mum has had her bag nicked" said the young teenage girl as she ran across the road to where I was standing in full view of anyone who may need my services.

I had to chuckle as I deliberately stood very close to the pedestrian access signpost which pointed to the various amenities, including toilets, post office, chemist, clock and car parks. You could guarantee ninety five per cent of questions would relate to the whereabouts of one of them, but rather than read the sign it was more fun to speak to the policeman. With a grin and a pointed finger, first to the signpost, and then in the relative direction I sent people on their merry way. But this was different, at last!

As I followed the girl across the road to one of the many food outlets along the seafront I could see a middle aged couple with two more kids who I would guess maybe a ten year old and an eight year old pair of brothers remarkably alike. The mother, a plump woman in her mid forties was very distressed, surrounded by several suitcases and smaller bags, with dad standing to one side with his hands folded across his chest in a defiant manner; she was obviously giving him a roasting.

The family were not well dressed and I guessed that whatever had been pinched would have not been of much use to the thieves, but was probably the families' own little fortune.

When I reached the forlorn little group, the mother launched into a tearful tirade of woe, how they had only left the kids for a few minutes to pop in and buy some food, only to come out to realise one of her bags had been taken. The kids had got chatting to a couple of teenage girls who they thought were locals, asking about where were the best places to go in this tiny godforsaken town they had been dragged to on holiday. It was only when, as one had kept them all looking away from their bags that, the other one had disappeared along with a bag.

The problem was, they had hit the jackpot, that was the bag containing all the holiday money, they had just arrived for the week and hadn't even been to their pre booked accommodation.

Now, I had been scanning the crowds before the incident.

The town was bursting with visitors as the warm summer sunshine brought not only the day trippers but also the regular holiday makers out in droves. It was amazing how the sunshine transformed the moods of everyone, the holiday makers were happy, the shop keepers were happy, and the local beat bobby was happy in the knowledge that he could walk about his beat not worrying about the weather.

A daytime duty was great on foot, provided the weather was good. Otherwise it was quite a guessing game as to what to wear to be ready for whatever the British weather saw fit to throw at the unsuspecting bobby out on the beat often quite a way from his station. This was where the joys of chatting to shopkeepers and building up rapport with the many kindly people who enjoyed having a bobby pop in for a chat and a cuppa; they loved to see if they could squeeze out the latest gossip, scandal or facts of recent small town occurrences.

It has been said, if you want to know what to wear regarding weather, see what the police are wearing. This was where, in the daytime, the trick was to check the forecast, and initially go out armed with whatever clothing may be thought necessary. First stop would always be a trusted tea spot central to the beat where you could arrange to leave your overcoat or raincoat, to be collected at the first sign of inclement weather.

Likewise, on the few times it was possible, you could leave your tunic if you could get away with patrolling in shirt sleeves. The old police "tardis" type boxes used to be used for just such a thing, but with the advent of police radios the contact point of the beat phone was no longer required.

I knew the majority of the local problem teenagers, there were very few female ones, and I had not seen any of the usual suspects in the area. I suspected that the offending girls were from the bigger neighbouring town, drawn there for the precise purpose of easy pickings from relaxed and unaware holidaymakers.

As I took descriptions of the offending girls, at least the best that the kids could give me, I groaned inwardly as I knew they would have immediately swapped tops to totally confuse identification. If nothing else, I could assume that they had come by bus, so details were passed to other patrols nearer the bus station to keep an eye out for them.

But, there was a big plus factor in this. If they were not locals then they would not know the area very well, so would not have a good local knowledge, so they would dump their unwanted pickings nearby.

I was as sympathetic as I could be as I took details of the brown shopping bag with zip top. It contained a black purse close to the top, which on reflection the lady recalled taking out of the bag to get the money for the food, but she had definitely put it back in and zipped it up securely. This was obviously what had been seen by the girls. The rest of the bag contained lightweight raincoats, but at the bottom of the bag was the bounty, a red clasp purse containing four hundred pounds cash for the week ahead, plus their return train tickets and house keys.

Luckily she remembered the accommodation address which I recognised to be one off the town centre about half a mile away.

I took down full details for the crime report, who they were and where they were staying.

I told them that in my experience the bag was more than likely to have been dumped nearby minus any valuable contents. I would do what I could, and always being the positive person that I am, said that I was sure it would turn up soon, but not to hold their breath for the money.

If it was just opportunist theft then there was not likely to be a problem with the keys. It turned out another older teenage son had remained at home to study for exams so someone was at their house, and that there were no address details in the bag.

In the brief time that I had taken the details the crowds around them had changed many times. Nobody would have thought twice to see the girl walking off with the bag, so I thought it pretty well useless to even start asking about for witnesses. All I had to go on was the direction the girls had run off towards.

Many times when a theft is reported it is considered that the owners are very unlikely to see their property again, by the very nature of the theft. I was always a positive thinker, and "never say die until I had given it my best shot" was my work ethic.

The region off the shopping area was a maze of alleyways; anyone could have been taken. A good eighty percent were dead ends which always played into the policeman's hands if chasing someone not familiar with the area. Could it be I would strike lucky and catch the girls coming out of an alleyway?

I had a good feeling about this one. It is said that a hunch is a sixth sense, and a "copper's nous" goes even one better. To follow a gut feeling, trust what it is telling you and come up trumps is a very special feeling. It is placing the trust in the hunch being right, and having the courage of your convictions to follow it through.

My first choice of alleyway made me realise, if I was going to search thoroughly I would lose time if I was going to find the girls, so I decided that a brief visual check of the area would be my best option.

After having checked a dozen of the alleyways and back yards without success I decided the trail had gone cold for the girls, so it would be a case of playing hide and seek. Now, if you were a couple of teenage girls in possession of a stolen bag, where would you take a chance to look inside, and where would you dump it?

Logic said it would be in a closed alleyway so no chance of being surprised by someone coming the other way.

I started to look more closely in each yard, and realised immediately that I was on a lucky streak; the bins were all empty as the collection had been earlier in the day. "Great" I thought to myself "no need for gloves just yet." I would have appeared unusual wearing gloves in this weather. When I met anyone during my search I quickly asked if they had seen the girls, giving a brief description, but no-one recalled seeing them.

As I completed searching alleyway after alleyway, yard after yard, something inside me kept driving me forward. It was like the game itself, only without someone saying warmer, colder and the like. I held on to my gut feeling which seemed to be telling me I was near to the jackpot. I had used this intuition several times before and had not been disappointed.

Bin after bin, nooks and crannies, doorways and window ledges, my search failed to find what I was looking for. The description was a brown shopping bag with zip top, there could be several variations on a theme, what shade of brown, how big, how tall, wide, etc etc . . . . that's it!!!!

"Eureka" I thought. As I was leaving yet another of the yards, some unknown sixth sense made me look upwards. Above my head some ten feet off the ground was a foot wide ledge, and there, lying sideways, was a brown shopping bag!

"They obviously threw it up there" I thought, "how am I going to get in down?"

I looked around and saw a long clothes prop lying against the wall at the top of the yard.

With a little bit of deft arm work I hooked the strap and brought it tumbling down into my waiting arms. The zip was open and a small black purse fell out as it landed. I picked it up and looked inside the purse but found it empty. I knew better than to start rummaging through the bag, you never know what might be in there!

Trying not to sound too excited I radioed control and asked them to contact the guest house the family had booked into. I assumed that without money they would not have dashed out anywhere, and at least the mother would have wanted to unpack a bit if they were able to stay. If they were there then could someone come down to the police station to see if the bag which I had found was the one which had been stolen?

I received a call a few minutes later to say they were on their way, and quickly arranged to be picked up by a passing patrol car. It would have looked odd to see a policeman in full uniform walking through the town centre carrying a full shopping bag!

I had just arrived at the back door of the station as I received a call on the radio; there was a family waiting for me in reception.

As I brought them through the security doors and ushered them into the interview room, there was a gasp of amazement from the Mum as she saw the bag on the desk, it was obviously the right one!

Only then did I become aware of the colour of my hands, they had obviously got dirty through lifting so many bin lids. I made my apologies just in case.

"The small purse was on the top when I found it" I said, "I haven't looked any further."

You would think it has contained the crown jewels as the mother grabbed the bag, reached down to the bottom and pulled out a wrinkled yellow cagoule with great gusto. Her eyes were nearly bulging out of her head, and I was aware that the whole family appeared to be holding their breath.

She shook the cagoule over the table and a large, fat, red clasp purse fell onto the surface with a resounding thud. It did not take a genius to realise that it was heavy, but as she snatched it up off the table and popped open the clasp, it opened to reveal a sheaf of bank notes.

"My god, it's all here!" she shouted, jumping up and down and hugging the rest of the family. She burst into tears and went to give me an impromptu hug, which in the circumstances I felt I deserved but could not return due to my filthy hands. As I extricated myself from the embrace the father grabbed my hand in his big paws and shook it vigorously, oblivious to the mess.

"How on earth did you find it?" the father asked.

Just then the door opened as the duty sergeant Chris Hobson walked in, wondering what the heck was going on, what was all the shouting and cheering about coming from an interview room?

The mother waved the purse jubilantly above her head and said with tears in her eyes—"Your copper here has just saved our holiday, he's fantastic!" and then planted a big soppy kiss on my cheek.

The whole family were beaming from ear to ear and seemed like they had won the lottery, so Sergeant Hobson realised there was not a problem at all.

"Here, let me give you something for your trouble" said the Dad as he reached into his wallet.

Eeeek! The one thing that was a big no-no was for an officer to accept any gifts, so I quickly explained that it was not allowed, but if they cared to make a donation in the Widows and Orphans Charity collection box on the front counter they were welcome to do so.

Had the sergeant not been there I may also have suggested a letter of thanks to the Chief Constable might go down a treat, mega brownie points for me, but I decided against it!

It turned out there had only been a couple of pounds and a bit of loose change in the small purse on the top of the bag.

Now there were the politics of the case, the constant battle to keep the crime figures in check. Yes a crime had been committed, but for the sake of a couple of quid, did they still want to report it? Because no offender had been traced and was never likely to be so, it would go down as an unsolved theft.

They were just so pleased to get their holiday spending money back that there was no need for a theft report or crime number. So, happy customers thinking that the police were not a useless bunch after all, young thieves who would never know what they had missed out on, and no unsolved crime report.

"That's the way to do it" I thought as I waved the family goodbye, noting with gratitude the banknote I saw the father pass to the youngest boy, who stood on his tip toes to put in the collection box on the counter.

"It is days like today which make the job worthwhile." I thought to myself as I went off to wash my hands.

Chapter Seventeen

The afternoon shift had quickly passed as I made a valiant attempt at clearing my ever growing mountain of an 'IN' tray. Alongside all the routine incidents that were dealt with on the streets and their associated paperwork, it was common practice for the shift sergeant to share out all the "paper checks" which came across his desk.

Included in this are the application for, or renewal of, firearms and shotgun certificates, and also outstanding arrest warrants issued for numerous reasons but mainly for non appearance at court after a person had been bailed to attend.

Every officer had his own pile to get through, but the warrants were the biggest pain because, out of necessity, if a suspect knew he was wanted he made it difficult to be found, getting relatives to lie on his behalf about his whereabouts. So, sometimes it was just pure luck that an officer would see the person out shopping or out drinking (somehow they thought that made them invisible!)

Ironically, I had in my possession a warrant for non appearance for a guy who was affectionately known as Big Jack. As a child he had "giant syndrome", and although his parents were normal size, he grew so fast that by 10 years old he was 5 feet tall, but by 17 he was an astonishing 7 feet 2 inches, and as is often associated with that condition he was considered learning impaired and was not the brightest of the bunch.

He was easily led astray by his "mates", who, because of his size, used to dare him to do things to show off his strength. Many of these got him into trouble and brought him to the attention of the law.

I knew him well, but I had always made a point of dealing with him fairly and found that Jack held me in a higher state of respect than some of my other hot headed colleagues.

The early evening pint is always a great leveller for the stresses and strains of daily life, and Big Jack loved nothing more than to pop in to his local on the way home.

Unfortunately being a creature of habit can be a downfall, and in this case gave me a realistic chance of finding him. Let's face it, at his size it was difficult for him to hide in a crowd anyway.

As I made my way back towards the station after having successfully completed several shotgun licence enquiries I thought, "maybe I'll find Jack at the Shoulder of Mutton pub" and headed in that direction.

There was method in my madness, if I could get to him before he had had chance to drink too much then the whole procedure would be a lot easier. When a giant does not want locking up, that causes numerous problems!

I approached the rear yard entrance to the pub where I could see directly into the rear bar (no lounge for Big Jack) and sure enough there was the huge outline of my quarry.

I quickly stepped back out of view and called the control room on my radio. The one annoying thing, an unusual quirk of science and nature, was that this particular area was very bad for radio transmissions, but was unfortunately a flashpoint for various public order offences particularly at night, often when help was needed most.

My call was received in a broken crackle and I had to move further away to get a better signal. I requested transport for a prisoner but never said who it was going to be. Without a second thought when I was told that a car would be with me in five minutes, I then asked permission from supervision to enter licensed premises.

Not always an operational requirement, it was a sensible "cover your arse" manoeuvre as all sorts of allegations can be made if an officer is seen coming out of a pub at any time when in uniform. I quickly explained to the duty sergeant that I had the warrant for arrest of Big Jack and could see him in the pub.

"OK" said Colin Shepherd, duty sergeant back at the station, "do you need any help?" he asked in a concerned manner, well aware of Big Jack and his antics.

"No, I'll be fine" I said, confident in my ability to deal tactfully with Big Jack without anything kicking off.

After all, the usual tactic of grabbing a villain by the arm and hauling him out would just not work with Big Jack! It would take at least four, if not more to overpower him, there would then be the nightmare of struggling to get him out of the pub and into transport.

No, this called for a totally different approach. I would have to "Ask" him to accompany me!!

I entered the pub through the back door, and as anticipated everyone fell silent in the small bar area, before some anonymous joker said "Ay up, fancy dress was last week!"

The fact that I kept my hat on as I entered the pub was an indication to the locals that this was not a visit to pass the time of day. I caught the eye of the barman whom

I knew well, glancing in the direction of Big Jack, and we connected mentally as to my reason for being there.

"Oh bloody hell!" boomed Big Jack's voice "can't a man enjoy a pint? I heard you'd been looking for me."

I looked directly at Big Jack, ever aware that whilst wearing my large police helmet I barely came up to his shoulder. The man had an enormous head adorned with a big wild mane of unkempt frizzy hair, long sideboards and long jutting square chin. He had several broken teeth in his wide mouth, which always reminded me of the big guy in the James Bond movies.

To my dismay I looked at the bar in front of Big Jack to see the white froth on a freshly pulled pint of best bitter just settling. There is one thing to arrest a man for something he knew he had done wrong, but quite another to part him from his pint. Add to that the clang of the till as I walked in, I knew it had been paid for! What better way to start a war.

For some people, being arrested in full public view would be a real embarrassment, but to the criminal fraternity like Big Jack it was a badge of honour. There was a game to be played here. Big Jack knew there was a warrant out for his arrest. It was not for me to announce to the world the reason for the warrant. This then provides the villain with a wide scope of embellishment to his story to be later regaled to his cronies as to the reason why.

Somehow non payment of parking fines or council tax did not have the same impact as robbery or assault!

"Now then Jack, how are you doing?" asked I carefully, watching intently to see how my appearance was going to be received.

"All the worse for seeing you!" snarled Big Jack, but he broke into a grin all the same.

"You know what's this is about, so let's get it out of the way and you can be back in time for the match on TV." I joked, all the time watching closely to assess the situation, aware that I had just told a little white lie.

The warrant was for failing to appear at court, so I knew that once in custody he would not be released until he appeared at court the following morning.

"I've just got a pint in, so you are going to have to bloody well wait" growled Big Jack.

Quick as a flash I saw a way to break this deadlock, playing to the hero's ego is always the best way.

"What's up Jack, are you losing your touch? They always reckoned you could not be beaten in a drinking competition, rumour had it you could get one down in three seconds."

You could almost see the cogs slowly turning in Big Jack's colossal head. Not for a second did he realise just what I was trying to do, but he dare not lose face in front of the other beer swilling buddies standing around, watching and listening intently.

"Huh, watch this then" said Big Jack as he picked up the pint of beer, dwarfed in the great paw at the end of his arm.

In the blink of an eye he put the glass to his lips and drained it in one single action, he didn't appear to swallow at all. To the cheers of his mates he casually put the glass back onto the counter and grinned from ear to ear at his achievement.

"Well done Jack, I see the rumours were true, that wasn't even three seconds!" I announced.

Suddenly the light of day dawned across the amiable giants' crooked face, his pint was gone and he had no reason to refuse to leave. "You clever bastard" he hissed at me, realising he has been outsmarted.

Just then my radio crackled into life. Although not too clear, I realised the transport had arrived.

"Taxi waiting outside Jack, come on, let's get this sorted out."

The giant shrugged his shoulders and muttered "better now than two in the morning", recalling last time his front door had been kicked in, after a drunken brawl on a Saturday night when he had put three visitors to the small town in hospital.

As we moved to the door, I quietly told Big Jack he was under arrest on a non appearance warrant. It was not necessary to caution him as nothing said would affect his circumstances. An officer must inform the person they are under arrest before being entitled to lay a hand on them forcefully without being accused of assault.

As we emerged onto the street we both stopped in amazement.

"You've got to be joking!" said Big Jack.

I stared in frustration as I saw that the "transport" was an officer in a small three door Vauxhall Corsa run around. My call for transport had not requested the van, but assumed the civilian radio operator would have sent it, even after having called to supervision she had not connected the dots . . . Obviously at that time of day, people were in for a meal, and the number of available vehicles was limited. I realised I had to act quickly so as not to upset the big guy.

Normal rules are that a prisoner cannot travel in the front of a patrol car, and they must sit in the rear behind the passenger seat to reduce the risk of an attack on the driver if no partition is fitted. Fortunately my colleague driving the small car got out, showing Big Jack that he was a tall six feet four chap who had learned to ease in and out of the small car.

"Tell you what Jack, why don't you get in the front?" I said, quickly sliding the passenger seat back as far as it would go. "It won't take long to the station; otherwise you are going to have to wait here for a long time for the van"

"Looks like no choice" grumbled Big Jack as he reluctantly squeezed himself into the car, the whole of the car appearing to lean over to the passenger side. I climbed into the rear seat from the drivers' side and the driver got in. It would have been impossible for Big Jack to get into the car if he had been handcuffed behind his back, and even cuffing his hands in front of him would not restrain him much due to his size. I wasn't even sure that the handcuffs would fit him.

As it was, Big Jack was scrunched up with his head pushed to one side and hardly able to move. It was a calculated risk which we had to take.

The patrol car pulled in to the rear yard overlooked from the control room, and they saw the amazing sight of the giant emerging from one side as the driver and I got out of the other. So, they knew the rules had been broken, but needs must.

The security doors opened and Big Jack had to stoop to get through into the bridewell area reception for prisoners. I noticed several other people being processed, and the last thing I needed was to keep Big Jack waiting. If he kicked off, everything else would go out of the window as we dealt with him. Fortunately just then Big Jack said loudly to no-one in particular, "I need a piss."

Due to previous recent problems the available toilet had been damaged and therefore not useable. The only other toilets in the area were situated in the individual cells.

I glanced towards the custody sergeant and then the board, seeing that there were two empty cells.

"Can we put Big Jack in number four for the time being Sarge?" I asked quickly, interrupting the never ending paperwork. There were sufficient details on the warrant to fill in the necessary bits on the custody form to allow Big Jack to be put in a cell, so the Sergeant nodded and tossed the big bunch of keys across.

"OK Jack, just empty your pockets and give me your belt" I said, knowing that in the urgency to go to the toilet Big Jack was less likely to prove awkward. He rapidly obliged, I made a quick check for hidden objects and led him to the cell.

"It's a bit busy now Jack, I'll get back to you as soon as I can" I said.

True to my word, as soon as the custody officer was free then I saw to it that Big Jack was properly processed. It was then that the terms of the warrant were read out to him and it was explained that he would appear before the magistrates the following morning after being held overnight.

Big Jack snarled at me.

"You lying bastard, you said I would be out in time for the match!"

"Sorry Jack, I didn't realise there was a retaining clause, but what do you expect if you can't be trusted to turn up when you are told to do so. You wouldn't be here now if you had turned up last time when you said you would. That's why we get you to sign when you are bailed, you promised us you would go to court at that time and you didn't."

I explained as carefully as I could without upsetting the big fella anymore.

Just as the paperwork was finalised and I was putting Big Jack back into the cell an urgent call for any available units came over the radio, a violent domestic at a familiar location. I just had chance to pick up my helmet as one of the patrol car drivers ran for the back door, I ran along as well.

The problem was not necessarily going to be the domestic itself, but the fact of where it was, all the neighbours felt it was their duty to interfere with any attending units trying to sort it out. You needed eyes in the back of your head there, which is exactly why I went along as back up, and someone to watch the police vehicles.

As expected when we arrived, not only was there a disturbance at number forty four, but neighbours from both sides were out as well. It was one thing for the council to put all the trouble makers in one area, but a nightmare to police.

Inevitably the arrival of more police units attracted the local kids, all brought up on a diet of police hatred and anguish, none of whom had any concept of acceptable behaviour. As always the plan was to get in and out as quickly as possible with the least amount of damage to vehicles or personnel.

The perpetrator of the violent domestic was one of the local druggies who, when high on anything, felt he could take on the world. I had even seen him try to bite a police dog once! He was taunting the two young officers who had arrived first. I could see them both rising to the bait and it was going to rapidly get out of hand.

I strode forward, straight past the younger officers and up to the front door where Mr Invincible was ready to take on the world. As I approached him the druggie, Sean Baltimore, slid a length of pipe which he had been hiding up his sleeve, into full view.

"Perfect" I thought. Up to that point I was a bit concerned about being accused of using excessive force, but now it was self defence. I had never drawn my truncheon in anger, my previous training in Japanese martial arts had always taught me to use any aggressors' weapon against themselves.

The one thing that it took young officers a lot of time, trouble and bruising to learn, was that anyone in a drug induced rage does not feel pain, except for two places. I had never yet been challenged over my methods, they may have been unorthodox and definitely not in the rule book, but never failed. He was stood in the doorway braced for a fight.

With one lightening kick I hit him hard, straight between the legs! It was enough to make everyone nearby gasp, but also enough to make him drop the steel pipe and drop his guard for the fraction of time it took me to get his arms behind him and the cuffs on.

"Needs must" I thought.

The guy started to kick and squirm, but it was enough to get him subdued so we could put him in the waiting van. A quick glance around the smashed up kitchen satisfied me that if nothing else a breach of the peace had been taking place, and was likely to recur.

I knew better than to ask the tearful wife with a thick bleeding lip whether she wanted to complain. If she had, she would retract the statement next day anyway. I checked that she didn't need any medical treatment and that the kids were OK, so I was out of there.

Heavy handed policing? No, an arrest had been made, the situation resolved.

"I'm sure those do gooders would have something to say" I said, as I jumped in the front of the van, "but it's not them that gets kicked and bitten."

When we arrived at the bridewell Mr Invincible had regained his universal powers and was prepared to fight anyone and everyone, even with handcuffs on. He couldn't be put in a cell with the cuffs still on, but it left a bit of a problem as to where to put him in his highly aroused state.

"Do you know what I'm thinking?" asked the custody officer as three of us were trying to stop Mr Invincible from trying to kick anything and everything. "I think we need to keep a cell spare, so he can go in with Big Jack for the time being."

"Oh boy, talk about the perfect solution" I grinned. He was dragged kicking and screaming to the cell door, marched in and held down as each officer made ready to let go. The cuffs were removed. We needed to be able to walk backwards and out of the cell without receiving any last minute kicks. Big Jack had stood up in the corner wondering what the hell was disturbing his little world.

The door slammed shut and as expected Mr Invincible launched a fierce attack at the thick steel. Mumbled noises came from within, and then a raised voice, and eventually a roar from a real giant "Pack it in!" It was only at that moment Mr Invincible turned to take on his tormentor. He stopped in his tracks, blinked and rubbed his eyes.

"The drugs must be making me crazy, this guy is HUGE" he must have thought.

It was enough to shut him up.

Chapter Eighteen

As I pedalled towards the station my mind was working overtime, how could I get to the kids sports day whilst still being on duty?

It always seemed to happen that sports day fell when I was on the afternoon shift. It always appeared to be sprung on me last minute and any arrangements to try to wriggle out of my shift fell through.

I decided the best way would be to come clean with Colin the duty sergeant and ask if I could have the foot beat which covered the area. Of course, the local community beat bobby had adjusted his duties so that he could attend at the school to provide crossing patrol and a visible presence.

Colin told me that I would be one of the area car drivers. "If you just happened to be in the area then it doesn't really matter where you park up, now does it?" he said with a wink.

"Cheers Sarge!" I said, knowing that the job would still come first.

I checked my in tray and noticed a request from Joe D'Arcy out on his rural beat. There had been an incident at his local pub way out on the moors the night before, a young lady had been injured and he needed a statement. I put the request with the rest of my paperwork and set about my beat.

The sports day was to start at two thirty so I couldn't really get stuck into anything before then. I cheekily parked on the school emergency access ramp, as most of the teachers knew me, and if I hadn't been driving then Robbie, the community bobby would be. We would be easy to spot.

The kids were very excited to see me in full uniform, telling their friends in loud voices.

I found Angela in a group of Mum's nattering about the usual stuff.

You could see the connection being made as several of them hadn't previously realised I was a copper. Fortunately the kids were at that age where they were proud of that fact, rather than the teenage response to shy away from being related!

I saw Robbie across the field and acknowledged him, pointing to the car just to let him know I was not stepping on his toes. He gave me the thumbs up in recognition.

The kiddie's races came thick and fast and fortunately there were no calls on the radio.

Just as things were dying down I caught the end of the loudspeaker announcement ". . . . so all the Dad's to the start line for the sprint."

I turned a deaf ear; I couldn't possibly be expected to run, full uniform and all!

Three noisy little voices thought otherwise and I was dragged reluctantly to the start line.

There were several of the other dads there, some in trainers and T shirts.

As it happens I used to be a very good runner, but with all my gear on I didn't really give myself a chance. My youngest said in a very loud innocent voice "But daddy, you must be fast to catch all the bad guys."

"No pressure then!" I thought as we waited for the gun to go.

BANG! I was off like a hare, determined to at least be amongst the front runners. To my amazement there was only one guy in front of me, and as we neared the finish line one huge burst of speed put me past him at the tape.

The kids were ecstatic, Angela was suitably impressed and cheers all round. My heart was beating so hard I thought it would jump out of my chest as I gulped for air. Just then my radio sparked into life.

"741, Can you attend a disturbance outside the "Lunchbox cafe" on Park Street?"

"10-4" I panted, trying not to sound dead on my feet. It was ironic that I couldn't stick around to get my winners medal but I asked Angela if she could do the honours.

I semi jogged across the field to the marked police car, and just for show put on the blue lights as I left in a hurry for Park Street, the kids will have loved that. I turned them off once round the corner!

Upon arrival at "The Lunchbox" a small group had gathered. It transpired that a disgruntled customer had been so disgusted with his food that he had refused to pay and walked out. The proprietor had accosted him and in his words "made a citizen's arrest."

In these circumstances things were not so clear cut. The offence of "making off without payment" had some overriding components which could change it from a criminal act to a civil dispute.

Yes he had complained in the café about the food, yes attempts had been made to rectify it, no he had not eaten it all, yes he had verbally stated he refused to pay and no, he did not run away but merely walked out.

It seemed to me this was definitely a dispute over quality and service. As I explained to the proprietor I also noted the increasing crowd since my arrival, informing him that it was not good for his business and we needed to settle this quickly and amicably.

The disgruntled customer knew his rights, he had done nothing wrong. He was prepared to pass on his details in case the proprietor wanted to pursue a civil case, but otherwise just wanted to get on his way. There was no further reason to detain him so I thanked him and sent him on his way. The proprietor "thanked me for nothing" in his words and went back inside.

There was no point returning to the sports field but I was pleased I had been able to attend. I was just around the corner from the address on the request by Joe for the statement.

It was the end house on a long stone built terrace. I knocked on the front door which didn't appear to have been opened in years, weeds growing across the path and spiders cobwebs across the door.

Just then a head popped out from the end of the terrace and a lad in his early twenties shouted,

"Can you come round the back please?"

I walked round and was invited into a small enclosed yard. I immediately spotted a cast iron two seat bench of good quality which seemed out of place amongst the other broken down bits of garden paraphernalia.

My "crime detector" mind kicked in as there had been a report of a similar theft only two streets away a few nights earlier. I remember the comments at the time were that it would have been heavy and unless a van had been used they would not have got far with it.

The lad looked vaguely familiar but I couldn't place him. His dark curly hair was past his shoulders, he had an athletic body and deep tan with several tattoos, and he was sporting what appeared to be two weeks growth of an attempt at a goatee beard.

"I guess you are here for the statement" he said, indicating for me to step inside.

As I entered the cluttered kitchen I saw a young lady sitting in the corner chair, her left leg wrapped in white bandages supported on a stool. As I walked nearer, although she did not have any makeup on, the lady in question was naturally very pretty. Her bright blue eyes shone in her perfectly toned face and she flashed a welcome smile.

It turned out they had been at an event up in Joes' local pub the night before, the lad being a mobile DJ. That's when I remember having seen him at some distant party. She had tripped and fallen on a glass and gashed her leg open. Along with the rest of her body I could see she was a very shapely young thing.

She mentioned that she was a model, and of course any scarring to her leg would be a disaster for her future career. I could see the basis of a large compensation claim looming, but made sure to keep the statement to the facts.

I obtained all the details I needed, quickly jotting his name down as well for possible future contact. Bob Carpenter seemed to be a bit reserved in a strange sort of way, but was cordial and polite.

With all the paperwork completed I made my way to the rear door, noting that Bob closed it immediately behind me. I had a long hard look at the bench as I walked past, noting a small maker's disc in the centre of the top horizontal spar, well painted but still visible "Bakers of Cleardale".

I returned to the office for my break and took the chance to look up the crime report for the bench. There was no mention of the maker in the report, so I phoned the complainant and asked if they could recall anything more for the description. Sure enough, mention was made of the plaque but they could not remember the inscription. It was however stamped underneath with their post code DY2 4GY.

There was just enough time to have a chat with the local community bobby who happened to be in the office, it was Brian Collins who had returned to work after his embarrassing operation.

"Do you know this character Bob Carpenter on Railway Terrace?" I asked.

"Oh yes, where would you like me to start?" he smiled.

I explained why I had been round there and what I had seen.

"He's a bit of a lad," Brian continued, "a womaniser, petty thief, dabbles in drugs and has had many domestics with his various partners. He married the lovely Lorraine as he saw a high priced ticket to success, but I've been called a couple of times to domestics. He never marks her face, but I've seen a couple of handfuls of hair pulled out before now."

We checked in the intelligence file and were not particularly surprised to find a drugs enquiry marker next to his name. Drug squad were requesting all information to be passed to them and no unnecessary uniform dealings to be made.

Too late, I'd been round without any previous knowledge. I wandered down to the drug squad office on the off chance to see if anybody was about. I found Detective

Constable Peter Simons typing furiously onto the computer keyboard.

"Hi Pete, how's things?" I asked cheerily.

"Don't ask Tom, it's never ending." He glumly replied.

"Sorry, but I seemed to have stepped on your departments toes" I continued.

I explained about my visit, about the bench and my findings. If the bench was indeed the stolen one it would give them due cause to search his house for other stolen goods. If they just happened to find drugs in the search then hey presto!

"We're expecting a big shipment to hit town on Saturday Tom, could you leave it with us until then?" Pete asked.

"Sure, I don't think he had any clue I clocked the bench so it is all yours," I said, happy to be part of the inter-departmental co-operation.

The rest of the shift passed in a blur of petty calls and paperwork and it was soon time to go home.

The next shift the following day was a split shift six p.m. to two a.m, giving extra cover for the Friday night. I had completed my first three hours and was called in to take over one of the area cars as Tommy McFarlane had got tied up with a couple of prisoners.

I gave up any thoughts of completing any more paperwork enquiries as the night became busy sorting out the numerous calls which seemed to erupt on a Friday night.

I had returned to the streets after a late meal break and parked the car just off the town centre. Just then the radio call came in;

"All units, 999 call received. Violent domestic dispute reported on Railway Terrace, complainant is a Lorraine Carpenter!"

"741 I'm just round the corner, ETA 30 seconds" I shouted into the mike as I started the car. I was literally there in about 10 seconds, dashed from the car, into the back yard and through the partially opened door, hearing screaming and crashing sounds from inside.

I froze in my tracks as I saw Bob Carpenter who had hold of his wife by her hair dragging her across the room. She was totally naked but was holding onto the house phone, obviously screaming not only from the pain of having her hair pulled, but also her leg was still bandaged and god knows how much that hurt.

He immediately let go and she grabbed the nearest cushion in an attempt to hide her wonderful body. I guessed they were both astounded at the speed of my response.

There was a distinct sweet smell in the room mixed with the smell of alcohol. I knew I was now treading all over drug squad territory but had no real choice.

His eyes were glazed and unfocused, looking somewhat confused. Just then I heard footsteps outside and realised back up had arrived. To my relief it was Pete Simons.

Lorraine made a dash to the door to upstairs as quickly as her injured leg would allow, giving all in the room an eyeful of her naked rear view.

I looked to Pete for inspiration. Do we just sort out the domestic, or do we show our hand.

"Now then Bob" Pete said, "you at it again?"

"None of your fucking business" he slurred, still apparently unable to focus.

"Seems like you're high on something" Pete continued, "where's the stash?" he queried immediately.

"Nowhere you would ever find it you moron" hissed Bob. "Get out of my house if you haven't got a warrant."

"I think we can do one better than that." Pete quipped with a slight grin in my direction.

He motioned for me to go look at the bench outside. I quickly went out into the yard, turned the bench over and sure enough, DN2 4GY was clearly stamped into the wood.

Knowing that young Bob may be facing several assorted charges, I didn't really want to get involved. As I entered the kitchen I gave a quick nod to Pete. As if on cue and without any prompting he told Bob that he was being arrested on suspicion of theft of the bench and cautioned him.

The look on Bobs' face was one of incredulity. He might have been expecting to be locked up on a drugs charge, a breach of the peace or assault, but not on theft,

"Aw, that was just a drunken prank" he groaned.

Just then more footsteps could be heard. I didn't recognise the two people in scruffy plain clothes who came in, but the uniformed officer with a trained drugs dog was one I had met at headquarters.

"We were on a stakeout nearby" said Pete, "nothing really happening but this call was too good to miss out on." He said enthusiastically.

I was happy to handcuff Bob and put him in the back of my car. He seemed a handful when beating up women, but was just a wimp when faced with someone of equal size.

The drugs officers had opened all the windows and the door, apparently to get rid of the sweet sickly smell of cannabis, to allow the drug dog to carry out a complete search unhindered.

Lorraine appeared fully dressed by the stairwell door, just in time to see me leading Bob out to the car. Her puffy eyes filled with tears as Pete explained why he had been arrested, why the dog was there, and he also asked if she wished to press any charges for assault.

"It looks like he's really done it this time "she said, "I don't think I need to bother."

I later heard that the drug dog made short work of finding quite a substantial stash of drugs. It turned out their information had been wrong, and the shipment had arrived a day early and Bob was in on the act. As the drugs had been found, Lorraine had apparently broken down in floods of tears, not knowing anything about them. She had grabbed a bag of clothes and decided to leave him there and then.

It used to amaze me how things just have a habit of falling into place.

Chapter Nineteen

During the brief but pleasant summery spell towards the back end of August it was at last a pleasure to be out on the afternoon beat. The sleepy fishing town was bursting with day trippers enjoying their day out and the numerous small shops were doing a roaring trade in everything you would expect at a seaside town.

Down by the harbour the strong smell of seaweed hung in the air as the tide was out, but on the turn, and it was beginning to warm up. I enjoyed being on foot in this weather, and as my orders were to show a presence on the street, that was exactly what I was doing.

I didn't mind being the walking signpost to help people as I derived a lot of pleasure from it. Many people like to ask directions, and I could also see parents encouraging their children to "go ask the nice policeman" a variety of questions. It was a good way for them to meet an officer in uniform, and I liked to encourage the interaction.

This was in stark contrast to the families of, let me say, the not so honest fraternity who would spit in the street as they walked past, unable to make eye contact but quite capable of grunting like a pig.

My radio broke into my thoughts as I received a report that one of the shop keepers had reported some shop lifting. I was only a few hundred yards from the premises, and knew full well that as I made my way towards the small glassware and crystal shop that it was more than possible I would pass the offenders, but without details and description I was powerless.

The shop was just off the Market Square, a small single room establishment cluttered with all sorts of fancy figurines and baubles. The elderly lady proprietor smiled briefly as I entered the shop, I could see the discomfort on her face as there were several customers in the shop.

It was the sort of place that is run more as a hobby, only opens when there were enough visitors in town, so not well known to me. She motioned me quickly into the small office at the back, not wanting to have an officer in the shop as she was the sort who thought it would drive away custom.

How on earth she could manage to keep an eye on everything at once amazed me, there was only one other middle aged helper out there. As I soon realised, she knew every item, price and the origin of all her stock. Unusually, she was able to give a very accurate description of the two suspected offenders. It was not the sort of place that would attract any young teenagers; her clientele were normally middle aged.

Her description of the two was very detailed. The man was about thirty three years old, muscular build, six feet two inches tall (she knew because of the height of the doorway) wearing a black leather jacket with collar length wavy black hair, a red shirt and a very distinctive pair of pin striped trousers which, she said, "looked most out of place."

The woman was only about five feet tall, slim with natural mousey blonde straight hair worn in a tight bun held in place with a distinctive ivory coloured hair pin. She also wore a black leather jacket which had tassels on the arms which appeared nearly new. It was closed so she could not see what was underneath, but she had a white silk scarf and blue jeans with distinctive brown cowboy boots. The man had been carrying a small khaki coloured shoulder bag.

They had paid a lot of attention to two figurines and a crystal ball paperweight. After spending a lot of time browsing they left. At the time both assistants were busy with other customers, but a short while later the proprietor realised one of the figurines and the crystal paperweight were missing.

There were no cameras in the store, and it was only the quick eyes of the proprietor who had noticed them missing, many other similar shops would not realise for quite some time that they were gone. I was sure the thieves would have thought so too.

I quickly took down all the details for the crime report and then passed out the descriptions of the offenders for the others officers out in the town.

Because they had both been wearing leather jackets on a sunny day, and the female had a scarf, I suspected that they may have arrived in town on a motorbike. The pin striped trousers were a bit of a mystery, so I could envisage a flamboyant eccentric with a bike to match. There was no mention of them carrying helmets, which would mean they would more than likely have used the left luggage lockers at the station, next to the main car park.

As I made my way in that direction, an urgent call came in. A body had been seen in the river on the slipway. I was literally a hundred yards away and could see that a crowd was already looking over the river wall. As I ran round to get to the slipway my one thought was to save a life, or if not then to get the body out of the way quickly, this was the last thing the holiday makers needed to see.

Amazingly two people who were on the slipway had not approached the body, with water lapping around it. It was of a female wearing a long coat.

"Strange" I thought, "anyone wearing that would be well waterlogged, how come she has come in on the tide?"

With these thoughts racing through my mind I ran to the water's edge, grabbed the shoulders of the coat and pulled her limp body higher up the slipway out of the water.

"Something is not right here" I thought as I bent down. Her eyes were closed, but no sign of bloating, and the skin on her hands and face was normal colour and texture.

As I bent down to see if there was any sign of breathing I swore blind the body twitched.

Hmm . . . Maybe not. I reached to the side of her neck to check for the carotid pulse, and POW!

The pulse was like an electric shock. Rapid and strong! What on earth was going on here?

I turned sideways and realised the two people who had just been standing there had come a little closer forward.

"She's still alive then?" said the tubby woman in a matter of fact high pitched voice. Half question, half statement.

"What's going on?" I asked quizzically.

"We saw her standing there for about ten minutes. Then she just walked into the water and lay down on the slipway. Someone must have seen her and called you." She said.

"What on earth is this all about?" I thought. I turned my attention to the woman lying on the slipway. I checked her mouth for obstructions and tilted her head back to make sure the airway was open, but even as I bent down to listen for any breathing she coughed a mouthful of water. Her eyes were still closed. I lifted one of her eyelids to reveal her pinpoint sized pupil. With this limited knowledge I realised

I may be dealing with some sort of drug overdose. I shook her quickly to try to get a response but nothing.

"Ambulance required at the slipway" I called into my radio as I pulled her a little bit further from the water and put her into the recovery position. I was acutely aware of the large crowd all peering over the railings and walls nearby, at least pleased that this one was alive. The last time I had cause to pull a body out of the water, all the rotten skin and flesh had slipped off the bones, fortunately it had been early morning and not in full view of any holiday makers.

I did not recognise her, could not see a bag, so I started checking her pockets for any form of identification. I found a small purse with a bit of change and a return train ticket to Kendal. Now that was bizarre! If she had come with the intention of committing suicide why buy a return ticket?

The ambulance staff arrived and I related what I knew. They could not say if it was an attempted suicide, if it was an overdose it may be a cry for help, but they would need to check to see if the symptoms were related to other ailments. With no identity to go on, I would leave her in their capable hands. I had a quick look around to see if there were any discarded pill bottles or foils but couldn't see anything.

As they stretchered her away I had another quick word with the couple but they couldn't shed any more light on the incident. I was very sceptical. Return ticket, incoming tide, and a lot of people around. It was almost certainly a cry for help. I dusted off the sand from my uniform and decided that there would be no need to go back to get changed, I hadn't got my feet too wet but guessed the salt water would ruin the polished shine on my boots.

My mind went back to the shoplifting couple. I decided to take a look over by the railway station on the off chance that I might stumble across them. With the best intentions

I headed in the right direction, but time after time I was stopped by people enquiring about the "lady in the river" always keen to get a juicy titbit of information. As I didn't know anything, I couldn't tell anything, "alive but not kicking" became my stock response.

Traffic was beginning to get busy as the late afternoon crowds started to make their way homewards. When I reached the car park there were about twenty motor bikes in the dedicated parking area, the usual crowd of enthusiasts looking at the various high power machines. One in particular was drawing a crowd, all chrome and handlebars, a chopper unlike any others I had seen, very much built for style.

"If ever there was a bike to ride wearing pin striped trousers, then this would be it!" I thought to myself. I quickly moved away to a vantage point where I could watch the bike but also the comings and goings of the holiday makers.

I saw the car coming towards me from the car park. The occupants were an elderly couple who were obviously just setting off home. As I walked into the middle of the road to stop the car, the startled old man hit the brakes, and as such I had to do a frantic dive in front of his car.

The object of my focus had just been propelled forward off the roof of the car and was about to hit the bonnet as I lunged towards it, catching the expensive looking camera before it bounced. My actions attracted a few cheers as I straightened up. The look on the old man's face was a picture in itself as I handed the camera to him through the open window.

Not wanting to hold up the traffic, as no explanation was necessary; I merely said "have a safe trip home" as I waved them past.

"Another good deed for the day and a happy holiday maker" I thought to myself, considering the alternative would have been a damaged camera after the first turn at speed, it would no doubt have been crushed by passing cars, and the old folk would just assume their camera had been stolen. These things happen after a long day.

The bike was still there with no sign of the couple of suspects. I walked along slowly, trying not to look at the town clock on the top of the station, it was a sure fire way to make the afternoon go slower, as the firsts pangs of hunger were starting, I knew it would be a while yet before my allocated break time.

One thing you could usually count on, the closer it got to break time, the more likelihood of something happening to stop me getting there.

As if by magic, from within the streaming crowd approaching me, the couple answering the description emerged right in front of me. It was as if I had been given a picture of them, the descriptions were perfect.

In the blink of an eye I was stood in front of them and quietly asked them if I could have a word. I indicated to the opening of a small alleyway to their right which they obligingly stepped into. The man stooped down as if to tie his shoelace as the young woman stood in front of him.

Just then a sixth sense triggered inside me, "the coppers nous," as I glanced down just in time to see a crystal glass ball rolling down the alleyway away from them. Now I knew the alleyway was a dead end, so as long as they were between me and it, they had nowhere to run. Seeing the ball rolling away short circuited the need for me to make any exploratory enquiries and I told them both they were under arrest on suspicion of theft.

The man was obviously going to say he just happened to kick the glass ball and it had nothing to do with him. I stood my ground and radioed for transport for my two prisoners, I would lay good odds that the figurine would be inside the bag.

I reckoned that if they had come in a vehicle the male would have the keys, so if they wanted to put up a fight or run, I would hold onto the man, the woman wouldn't get far.

They seemed to realise that and neither made an effort to run. I needed to keep an eye on their hands so that the figurine, if it was in the small shoulder bag, did not get dumped as well. Only once the transport arrived and they were safely inside did I open the bag in front of them. There sure enough was the figurine, wrapped loosely in a scarf, along with several other items. The fact that none of them were wrapped was a dead giveaway that they were likely to have been stolen, nobody would sell them loose like that.

Both of the suspects were well spoken and the quality of their clothes suggested to me that they were professionals. I knew the sorts I normally dealt with, these two had an air of confidence about them, and I could see why. Trying to trace the origin of the other articles would be nearly impossible, there were so many small shops to choose from and they would know it.

As the two were led out of the back of the van and into the bridewell area, I quietly asked Mick the driver to do a quick check of the seats, a routine often overlooked, but sure enough he pulled out a key on a Triumph motorbike fob which had been pushed down behind where the man had been sitting.

I confirmed that the van had been searched at the beginning of the shift, and seeing as no other prisoners had been in there, it was a safe bet that the key belonged to them. Mick needed no prompting to make an all important notebook entry to that effect.

"Bingo" I thought, "I'd bet my pension that key belongs to the chopper in the car park." I described the machine and asked Mick, out of earshot of the couple, to go check, as I led the couple into the cell area, they were not aware that the key had been found.

Warning bells were ringing inside my head. Surely they would have motorbike helmets somewhere, more than likely in a left luggage locker. If they had helmets in there, what else would I find?

First of all I needed the locker key. Without it we wouldn't be able to access any locker for the mandatory twenty four hours, and I would need to have charged them by then.

Yet again I would bet my pension that the woman had the key. The couple would know that this would literally be the key to their freedom and would not surrender it at all costs.

A female officer was called in to the cell area as they both needed to be searched. Neither of the prisoners was forthcoming with anything other than basic information and I could sense this was going to be like pulling teeth. I didn't believe the details being given were even correct.

A brief search of the man revealed only the usual contents of pockets, nothing incriminating. I needed to get the couple separated quickly, but I expected they would have their story so well rehearsed that it would come out as second nature.

The female officer took the woman into a cell for a search. As I was booking the male prisoner in, the WPC came out with a slight shake of the head. Nothing found.

At that I realised there was going to be several ways to play this. Keep them separated, play them off against each other.

If my hunch was correct, I would have the ace up my sleeve. If that key fitted the bike, then enquiries at the neighbours of the registered keepers address would soon get a description, maybe a couple of names.

Hit them with that, neither of them knowing where the information had come from, each would think the other had grassed, and hey presto they would be on their way. There is no such thing as honour amongst thieves. As soon as one thought another had squealed, the gloves were off and it was everyone for his or her self.

The details given on the custody record appeared genuine enough, and there was no trace of convictions for either one of them, but that came as no surprise. The man had given the name Tony Whitehart, and the woman was supposed to be his wife Julie, both giving an address in the next big town.

There was no way that CID would be interested in something small like this, but I needed some female assistance as the WPC who had done the search was on day shift and about to go home. Maggie, in CID, was apparently twiddling her thumbs as I wandered in. I explained the situation, mentioning the bike and the as yet to be discovered locker key and she seemed pleased to be able to help.

Mick appeared at the door to the custody area as I returned with Maggie, a beaming smile on his face.

"I don't know how you sussed it, but it fitted like a dream, fired up straight away."

"Eureka!" I thought, now we really have something to play with.

"Maggie" I said urgently, "I need you to come down hard on this lass. She is not as cocky as he is. If we get the bike checked out, I can virtually guarantee it will be registered in his name, it is too much of an ego boost for him to cover up. If she thinks he has softened up already and is making her take the fall because she has the key to the locker, it should spook her into giving it up."

"OK, let's get the bike details" said Maggie, and within minutes we had the registered keeper details on a printout.

"So, it belongs to Peter Whitehart, registered at a different address. I bet he has given us a relatives details who is squeaky clean" I said, "let me just try something."

I went to the cell where "Tony" Whitehart was sitting on the bench. Without opening the door, I opened the hatch and shouted, "Peter, come here a minute!" Seconds later the face of "Tony" appeared at the hatch.

"Thought so" I said to him. "She is singing like a good 'un'."

I closed the hatch grinning to anyone and everyone around; having planted the seed of doubt in the prisoner's head I wondered how quickly the fabricated story and identities would collapse.

The interview with "Julie" started slowly, with Maggie taking the lead with the questioning. After several preliminary questions to test the water, Maggie looked directly at her and said:

"Peter has already told us all about you, so don't you think it's your chance to even the score?"

The colour momentarily drained from the woman's face, and then her cheeks flushed quickly, taken aback.

"He said it would be easy, how did you manage to find out?" she asked.

"Let's just say when he had the option of taking the rap for this; he decided that seeing as you have the locker key then you are more in for it than he is. Add to that when we seize his bike . . . ."

"How the hell do you know about the bike? What is this, how come you know so much?"

She began to get really wound up.

"Don't you realise, we've been watching you for a while. Don't you think it is about time you saved yourself instead of letting him get off scot free?" asked Maggie in a very concerned but defiant way.

"OK, OK, I've got the key. It's hidden where you'd never find it and I'm not getting it out here and now" she hissed.

I took that as my cue to leave the interview room. The tapes were stopped and I went outside. Maggie came out a couple of minutes later holding the key lightly between two fingers as she crossed over to the hand basin at the back of the desk She briefly rinsed the key, dried it on a paper towel and passed it to me.

"You check out the locker, I'll carry on the interview" smiled Maggie.

Locker 238 in the station left luggage area revealed not only matching motorcycle helmets, but also numerous other items, some quite expensive looking. Now, if "Julie," or whatever her name was, continued singing, hopefully a few shops might be identified.

There were also a set of house keys which I assumed would fit the registered address of the bike. Depending upon how these interviews went, we could well be going for a drive.

Searching of premises relating to stolen items was now common place, and provided that there was no alarm system or vicious guard dog in the premises, we could be back before dark.

When I returned to the station I knew by the look on the custody officer's face that things had taken a turn. The woman had been placed in a cell; Maggie was nowhere to be seen.

It turned out that once Maggie had got her real details and ran them through the PNC; a flagged marker came up with reference to the Regional Crime Squad No 2. The marker linked to a Peter Whitehart, wanted in connection with numerous illegal gaming and fraud activities. This was the chance they had been looking for, to gain legitimate access to his house without requiring a search warrant.

RCS colleagues demanded to take over the investigation from there, and officers were on their way over. It was going to be taken out of my hands. It looked like an innocent day out at the seaside and a bit of petty thieving had well and truly cooked their goose.

As it would take some time for them to arrive, I took the chance to sneak off for a bite to eat before making my statement and bagging up the property.

The recovered property was eventually returned to as many owners as could be identified, little did the lady in the glassware shop realise what a fantastic job she had done, the couple were later sentenced to many years in prison on numerous serious charges.

Chapter Twenty

When the night shift came around I always felt a strong mixture of eagerness and apprehension. I was very much a night person, as in enjoying the clear roads and lack of people.

I always felt a deep sense of responsibility that I should be the one out and about protecting life and property whilst the majority slept. My main reason in joining the police was to help others. If that then meant tackling villains, yobs or irate housewives, so be it.

Winter night shifts were long, bleak and cold. Summer nights were short and light. Although I worked the same number of hours, it always amazed me how the psychological approach to the duty could seriously affect the enjoyment or otherwise.

Tonight was a balmy early summer night. As I commenced my foot patrol on a beat just off the town centre I quietly wondered to myself what tonight may have in store.

There was a light westerly wind blowing which gave a slight chill to the warm air. From my vantage point on the cliff road I could see the surface of the Irish Sea rippling on the incoming tide, only a few clouds to spoil an otherwise idyllic sunset.

Warm summer evenings did nothing to clear the streets. As the drunks and slightly less intoxicated were eventually prised out of the various watering holes around the town, they were never in a rush to go home.

I often thought that alcohol ought to have a big warning on the bottle "Beware, drinking this will make you think everyone else is deaf"

Too often complaints arose because someone worse for drink was making a noise, whether it was singing at the top of their voice, shouting to their mates a few feet away or kicking an empty can down the street.

An instant measure of how much they had had to drink would be to ask them to quieten down. Some smiled sweetly saying "Shorry hofficer!" and staggered on their way.

Others thought it hilarious to put a finger up to their lips and say "Shhhhhhh" in a forced whisper as loud as the original noise.

Yet again others would stop, blink a few times, and carry on as if you did not exist.

Windows would be open due to the balmy night, meaning if there was a noise inside it would carry on the night air to annoy the neighbours. Not only could this be music, but babies crying or couples arguing. Likewise, noises on the street would wake people inside the houses.

Add to that the stuffy atmosphere inside the houses and tempers soon frayed. A little bit of consideration for others would go a long way to solving the problem.

Strangely, weekdays noises never seemed to cause the same level of complaints as those on a weekend. Maybe then there was more noise, particularly if it was the football season, or maybe people were less tolerant having had a few to drink themselves.

Either way, I knew that, for the first few hours at least, I would more than likely be dealing with a few complaints before the night was through.

As I made my way along the coastal road all seemed quiet. Various groups or couples were slowly making their way back to the numerous hotels and bed and breakfast places along the strip. My thoughts were interrupted by the radio.

"741—there is a report of a jumper at Wycliffe Hotel, can you attend?"

"10-4" I replied, quickening my pace to the location only some three hundred yards away.

I knew the hotel, a grand Victorian rambling building which had seen better days. The owners did their best to keep it in a good condition but time was against them. I also knew it was five stories high with those adequately large sandstone balustrades around the upper floor outer edges.

The town did not have many high rise buildings, and hence not many occurrences of attempted suicides by people jumping from them. There were some very high cliffs nearby which tended to attract the serious ones.

So, what could I expect to find when I got there? It immediately went through my mind that this would be a domestic, some hysterical woman threatening to jump off the top of a building because she had had too much to drink and witnessed an innocent birthday kiss to her husband by a friend that had been blown out of all proportion.

"I'm going to jump so don't come near!" I heard a young male voice shouting as I came around the corner. I instinctively looked high up towards the roof line but saw nobody.

"Don't think you can stop me!" I heard the shout again.

This time I had chance to locate the origin of the noise.

"What the . . . . ???" I thought.

To my amazement, there, standing on the window ledge, back pushed against the window was a lad in his mid twenties threatening to jump . . . . but he was on the ground floor!!!!!

To the very small group of people who had been attracted to the scene, his antics raised a few giggles. The fact that I had arrived had not apparently registered with the youth, who was making his comments to nobody in particular.

The hotel night receptionist approached me and said:

"For goodness sake will you get him down, he's giving the place a bad name!"

"Oh what will the neighbours think?" I thought pitifully, public image coming a lot higher up the ladder than a person's well being.

"Do we have a name?" I asked her routinely.

"He's called George, George Hamilton" said the flustered girl.

Although it was a ground floor ledge, it was still some seven feet from the rose bed below. I tried calling to George who took no notice whatsoever, except to keep making his threats.

I could tell that something was not what it appeared to be. If he had been drinking then he would more than likely have fallen off by now. Nobody appeared to be with him or showing any cause for concern. From that, and his inability to focus or return comments, I drew the conclusion that he was probably high on drugs of some sort.

Somewhere in the murky depths of my training I seemed to recall that some hallucinogenic drugs could cause the user to believe that even a kerbstone was a multi storey building, so heaven knows what the view from up there might be.

I made a quick call for the area car to meet me as I had formed a plan. I would take the blanket from the car, place it over the rose bushes, then go and talk to George from inside. Assuming no response to being talked back inside, it would be a matter of giving him a shove!

One thing for sure in my mind, this was not going to be a long standoff!

The car arrived, the blanket put in place, and I was led inside by the receptionist.

Fortunately the Yale lock had not been secured from the inside, so the receptionist let me into the room.

As I made my way to the window I was relieved to see it was a sash type one that slid up and down. It would have been calamitous if it had been an outward opening one which pushed the guy off the ledge immediately!

I eased the window up but the guy standing on the ledge never even noticed. I leaned out and said,

"C'mon George, let's get you inside and sort this out."

The totally spaced out George suddenly became aware of a voice from the Gods speaking to him, he didn't realise it was from by his left knee!

"I'll jump, I'll jump, just watch!"

I spoke quietly so only me and George could hear.

"You are so high on something that I bet if you jumped you would be able to fly. Go on, give it a try!"

I had made up my mind that a little push was all that would be required to gain the desired result; Mick was waiting just a few feet below to try to break the guys fall. The last thing I wanted was for George to fall backwards through the glass window or hit his head on the ledge.

Just as I was about to give him the required push, George spread his arms like an eagle and stepped off the ledge, letting out a blood curdling scream as he did so.

Within half a second he was on terra firma amidst the rose bed, blanket and waiting officer.

Something which always amazed me was how drunks or people high on drugs never felt pain, but likewise, probably because they were relaxed, never seemed to suffer serious injuries either.

I quickly made my way outside, obviously concerned about my flying charge. George was stood upright staring into space, not making any noise. He was swaying slightly, but as I got a closer look I could not smell alcohol, so I reckoned that I had guessed correctly.

Georges' eyes were staring ahead and he did not respond to any questions.

In these circumstances the persons' ultimate safety, and that of others, is paramount. If we had just dusted him off and told him not to be so silly, then it is very likely that he would try the same again, maybe from a higher point. The blanket power of arrest for preventing a breach of the peace was a good starting point and so I arrested him, searched and placed him into the back of the car for his own safety.

I re-entered the hotel and asked the receptionist if she could come with me back to Georges' room, as I needed to make a quick check to see if there were any indications inside the room as to just what drugs he may have taken.

The décor was a bit grand but faded a slight mustiness in the air, a general sense of the old grandeur of the place missing.

Nothing was immediately visible, I checked drawers and bathroom cabinet, toiletries bag and pockets of coats and clothes but found absolutely nothing. I could only assume that George had bought whatever he had taken whilst on his night out. He may have been a first time user who had experienced quite a radical trip.

Fortunately, as I was leaving, the receptionist had taken the trouble to pull out Georges' registration card. With all the legal hype over data protection and privacy, I knew that sometimes receptionists could be fiercely protective and it took forever to find out details of people involved in any incident.

However, if I just happened to read the card as it was lying on the reception counter as she was busy doing something else, then no, she knew nothing about how those details became known, after all, she had not told anyone!

With a quick grin, I wrote down the details and made my way out to the car.

I asked George if he had hurt himself but received no reply. There didn't seem to be any reason to take him to the hospital so we decided to take him to the police station. It was not Georges' lucky night. The sergeant was just about to go off duty, so the last thing he wanted was an uncooperative prisoner.

As I was booking him in I made a more detailed search of Georges' clothing and pockets, even his shoes—nothing. Throughout the process Sergeant Colin Shepherd kept asking the routine questions required but he did not receive one reply. Although I could provide the home details from the registration card there was nothing else to go on.

Colin needed to know if he was alright, if he was dependent on medication etc etc before he could lock him up in the cell for the night. What would happen if the guy was seriously mentally ill?

We knew he could speak, as he had been shouting from the window ledge. There had been no signs of routine medication in his hotel room. What were we going to do with him?

I had arranged for a person check on the PNC (Police National Computer) with the details we had, but nothing came up. Something didn't add up, this silence was very strange.

Now Colin and I were both old school coppers. We believed in a ways and means to achieve an end. It may not be politically correct in this day and age, but it got the job done. Threats to George had not worked. Pleas for information had not worked.

Colin knew something which might. As there were only the two of us in the custody area with George, there would be no witnesses.

George was slumped down on a hard plastic chair, his arms down by his side with the handcuffs off as there was no cause to expect violence.

Colin Shepherd asked George one last time if he was going to talk to them. Just silence.

With that I saw Colin clench a fist.

"Oh oh" I thought, "I don't want to be part of this."

"Don't worry" said Colin with a wink, "Watch this!"

What I saw next amazed me. Colin's fist shape then changed to reveal a different clasp. Where his four folded fingers had been clenched, the second finger second knuckle was raised, such that it protruded out from the rest.

This resulted in a bony protrusion, a bit like an arrow head in his fist. I couldn't for the life of me work out what he was going to do next.

Colin swiftly placed the clenched fist with protruding knuckle into the central area below Georges' ribcage, at the point when the ribcage joins. He then moved his knuckle down an inch, pressed in hard and at the same time upwards.

"Ow" shouted George, "stop it!" he screamed! His previous head lolling seated position changed suddenly to wide eyed half standing position clutching his chest.

"It works every time" Colin grinned, obviously proud of his actions.

"The pain is so intense you really would need to be on another planet or unconscious not to feel it" explained Colin.

"Police brutality" was a term ringing in my ears, but the effectiveness and required result was well worth remembering for the future!

"OK, so now we know you can hear us, and you can speak, let's have a few details" said Colin.

The fuzzy head on Georges shoulder seemed to clear with remarkable speed. As Colin asked his name and full address, the details given did not match those which had been on the registration card. We both glanced at each other. Ding dong, ding dong, alarm bells began to ring.

Why would anyone register at a hotel and give false details? They may be a terrorist, conman, thief, or a mistake?

Just then the slow cogs began turning inside my head. No wonder in his drug induced state the lad had not responded to being called George—I would bet my pension on that not being his correct name either!

Surprisingly, when people gave false details of name and address, they frequently used their correct date of birth, a strange quirk of human nature. You have to have a very good memory to be a complete liar.

"So, if you are not George, who are you?" I asked.

"Of course my name is George" he said indignantly.

"And I came down with the last rain shower." Colin said sarcastically.

"Sarge, can we lodge him in the cell whilst I check something out?" I asked tentatively, forever aware that the sergeant wanted to go home soon.

"Okay, but be as quick as you can."

George, or whatever his name was supposed to be, was placed in a cell and I went up to the control room.

The address he had given was in a town over two hundred miles away. I located the Police force and division it was in from the national database and called their control room number. By now it was nearly 1.00a.m. on a week day and things were likely to be quiet.

Once having cleared identity checks and received a call back, I asked their operator to do a "burgess list" check on the address given. This was the paper record from the census and council records which showed the full names of residents at a particular address.

Sure enough, one George Hamilton was listed, but was aged 63!!

Who else was listed at that address, mid 20's male?

"There is only one, a Philip Ashcombe. Hang on, that name rings a bell." The operator said, "I'll do some more checks and get back to you."

An agonising five minutes went past as I awaited the call back. When it came there was no great surprise to find that one Philip Ashcombe, answering the description of our George, was wanted on outstanding warrant for theft and obtaining money by deception. He had a distinctive tattoo of a spiders' web on the back of his left ankle.

As he had failed to appear it would not be possible for them to bail him again, an escort would need to be sent. Details were exchanged and arrangements made. As the prisoner was entitled to rest, and the time it would take for the escort to get there, I would have time to re visit the hotel and search his room again, this time on the grounds of looking for stolen goods.

A check of his left ankle confirmed his identity. The sergeant made the necessary arrangements with paperwork so the prisoner could be handed over and made a quick exit home. Only unless there were extreme circumstances would he return, as most things could wait until the early turn relief came on.

As myself and Mick the van driver returned to search the hotel room, I shook my head in amazement. Just how thick did these people need to be? The receptionist was not pleased to see our return as more late night guests were coming back and the fragile public image needed to be protected.

She was even more disappointed when I asked her to check what credit card had been registered with them. The details of George Hamilton came up, to which I informed her that this was likely to be subject of theft and non chargeable.

I then needed to confirm that she had the authority to make a statement of complaint on behalf of the management, and then obtained the statement as Mick searched the room.

Just as I was finishing the statement Mick returned to the foyer. He had packed everything in the room into the holdall brought by Philip or whatever his name was, but as he had prepared the bag something caught his eye. The corner of a credit card was showing partially hidden under the strengthening board in the base of the bag. As Mick fiddled to get it out he became aware of several others underneath.

There were five in all, none in the name of Philip Ashcombe. M'laddo had a few more questions to answer.

Due to the new rules on detention he had the right to his rest period, and I knew he would then be due for his escort back to his home town.

The only problem might be, if these cards had been stolen locally, I would need to chase up witness statements. We returned to the station with the bag and cards, I then had to find the contact details for the card registration services and see if they could tell me anything about the cards.

As usual I hit a blank wall. Here I was with credit cards belonging to some people who may not even know they were missing, and they wouldn't give any details. They said they would make their own enquiries but at this time there had not been any thefts reported. As an afterthought I called the Wycliffe receptionist just to check that the names on the cards did not match records of any of the residents.

"No" came the reply, life was not going to be that simple. Still, in the morning, if the cards had been stolen locally the detective sergeant would be happy to chalk up an instantly detected crime!

I also checked the recent lost property entries at the front desk, still nothing.

As I prepared my own report, statement of arrest and listed the apparent stolen articles found and seized in the hotel, I realised that the night had flashed past. I finished the paperwork in time for a quick once round the beat before knocking off.

It was going to be another sunny day; the early sunrise already began to take the chill out of the air as I made my way home. Last night's antics brought a whole new meaning to the term High Flyer!

Chapter Twenty One

Once again I found that I had been selected to do the office meal relief.

As previously described it was not particularly something I enjoyed doing as I would rather be out and about on the streets, but somebody had to do it.

Because the police station was in a small town it allowed certain privileges to the duty control room officers which are not available in the bigger towns, one of these being allowed to nip home for meals. As home was never far away it was considered alright for the duty office operator to go home in "half" uniform, i.e. police uniform under civilian jacket provided they carried a police walkie talkie radio at all times, and ninety nine percent of the time this system worked without a hitch.

Tonight was going to be different!

The evening meal relief was late as Pete Knowles, the regular control room operator, was working a split shift and would finish at one in the morning, so he went for his meal at eight o'clock. There was not much happening on this quiet Tuesday summer evening, a balmy night, still light outside, as I took over the reins and settled in quickly, even the civilian operator was upstairs having her break.

At twenty five minutes to nine an automatic alarm call came in for a car repair garage premises, and straight away I realised it was just around the corner from where Pete

Knowles lived. To save diverting another unit across town I called him on the radio, knowing he would be just about ready to return to the station, and asked him if he could have a look.

"No problem!" came the reply from Pete, a time served officer and ex forces veteran who would be using his own car. He had lived there a long time and was well known in the area.

After just a few minutes Pete called in to say he had found the front door slightly open, no sign of forced entry and nobody in the premises. He had spoken to a neighbour who had seen the owner leaving a short time before in a hurry, and it looked like he had not locked up properly.

I quickly found the key holder details in the alarm register, but noted with some dismay that the telephone exchange was in Cleardale some twenty miles away. I called the number which was answered by a lady who, upon hearing it was the Police took a sharp intake of breath.

"No" her husband was not home yet, he had been working late at the garage. Once it was established that there had not been an accident and the reason for the call was the alarm activation, she relaxed and explained that he would be on his way home,(before the days of widespread mobile phones) and she would have to tell him when he arrived to go straight back again.

I thanked her and, with heavy heart, called Pete to explain. This would mean that Pete would need to stay with the insecure premises until a relief could be found, which also meant that I would need to stay in the control room. As time moved on this would cross over the shift change and I could see my scheduled shift time ending at ten o'clock going out of the window.

I was just settling down to the idea of seeing out the shift in the control room when the 999 red telephone rang.

As always, all available ears pricked up around the station in anticipation of the forthcoming call. I listened as the automatic alarm generated message came through, glancing up at the clock to note time of receipt, then jotting down the details of the premises.

"Unusual" I thought. The premises in question were the other garage in town which also served petrol.

Just then Chief Inspector Jim Donaldson came in as I was replacing the receiver.

"Automatic alarm call from The Cherry Tree Filling station" I said, glancing again at the clock reading five to nine, and realised that I was following the same thought pattern as my boss when Jim said "Probably locking up early and got it wrong."

We both knew the garage closed at nine p.m. and on a quiet night the cashiers were known to be away on the dot, in their haste they could have set the alarm incorrectly.

"Have we . . . ." Jim's words trailed off as the direct link alarm connection from force headquarter burst into life.

"We have a panic button alarm activation at The Cherry Tree Filling Station on White Lane crossroads" was the urgent message. I acknowledged the call and immediately sent out a general call,

"All units: there is possible robbery in progress at Cherry Tree filling station! Respond with locations and ETA."

"642, I'll be there in two minutes" came the excited reply from Tommy McFarlane, the area car driver.

"1277 there in five" replied the traffic officer John Green.

"10/4" I acknowledged as Jenny the civilian operator came dashing in having heard the call out on the upstairs speaker.

In cases like this it was the civilian operator who would intercept all other calls so that the duty officer in the control room could concentrate on directing resources and handling the call. Jim Donaldson knew better than to get in the way and stood patiently by the window staring at nothing in particular. Two more bodies appeared in the control room, Detective sergeant Carl Peters and his sidekick Trev Cartwright.

"What we got?" queried Carl.

"Don't know yet" I replied.

"642, 10/5" came the breathless call as young Tommy McFarlane jumped out of his car as he arrived at the scene.

The 10/10 code is used widely by operators using nominated meanings; in this case 10/5 meant the unit had arrived at the scene. Unfortunately there wasn't a uniform meaning in differing forces, so in cross force border situations things could get confusing.

The location was on the outskirts of town on a major route. Any offenders would have a clear run out of town unless they lived locally, they would have a long run in open countryside in any direction to get away. The officers in the control room knew without an update there was little sense in taking any action.

"642 with update" called Tommy.

"Go ahead!"

"Confirm armed robbery. Single white male armed with a gun. He smashed the glass door on the way in and appears to have cut himself. No injury to staff except a little shaken" it was hard to hear him as the two tone horns of the arriving traffic car screeching to a halt drowned out the transmission. At least we knew Tommy was no longer alone.

"There has been a small amount of cash stolen. He made off on foot into the Parkside housing estate. Mid twenties about six feet tall, stocky build with short curly blond hair wearing a grey jogging suit, may be injured. Can we have dog section, SOCO (scenes of crime officers) and CID?"

"10/4" I acknowledged, my mind racing as I looked at the town map.

"We're in luck" I said, "He's boxed in by the railway line and the main road."

Because the town was so small, the addresses of the well known likely offenders were known, but nobody sprang to mind and definitely not on that estate. I nodded as Carl & Trev indicated they were on their way, at the same time I realised Jim Donaldson was in the process of contacting force control to request attendance of the nearest dog section and SOCO.

As speed is of the essence in these circumstances I realised I had to act fast.

"642, CID, dogs and SOCO are on their way. Can you tell the staff they will be with them very shortly, but I need you to go into the estate, see if there are any sightings, look for obvious blood trail. 1277 can you go down the main road to the bottom junction, if he doesn't live on the estate he will come out there."

"211 are you receiving all this?" I asked as I knew Pete Knowles had been waiting at the previous premises alarm callout.

"Sure am" replied Pete.

"I need you to go to the railway tunnel underpass at the top of Hunters Walk, if he needs to get past the railway line that will probably be his route."

"10/4 on my way" replied Pete, "what a difference this meal break was turning out to be." I thought to myself.

The underpass was a pedestrian access only; it was pure fluke that Pete had been on that side of the track in the right place at the right time.

"Dogs and SOCO en route" confirmed Jim "but ETA is twenty minutes at best."

As twilight was falling it was going to be a race against time, twenty minutes was pushing it, but the dog may stand a chance.

"470, CID to control" came Carl, still getting used to the fact he was no longer in a big town and that the control room operators could identify the collar number to a person.

"Just to confirm the offender appears to have been armed with a black pistol, unknown make. No shots were fired so not known if it's real, loaded or a replica. He was also carrying an army style rucksack."

"10/4"

I was just about to pass on the details to all units when the radio burst into life again.

Using the part of the 10/10 code meaning officer requires urgent assistance, I only got the identifying part call of "211" and silence. I knew where Pete had been sent, but also knew I didn't have any other units that side of the railway tracks.

It would take too long for them to drive round, so I urgently called 642 and 1277 to run through the underpass from their side as Pete needed help.

I was vaguely aware of Chief Inspector Jim Donaldson grabbing the supervision car keys from the hook and sprinting out into the yard. If an "officer needs assistance call" goes out there is only one protocol, anyone and everyone responds as seconds save lives.

I knew from painful experience that it is a waste of time trying to call the officer back, if they are in a situation where they require assistance, they are not likely to be in a position to answer their radio.

As the seconds ticked by you could cut the air in the control room with a knife, Jenny and I barely daring to breathe in case we missed a call.

Horrendous thoughts began to cross my mind. Will they need an ambulance? Will shots have been fired? Will they need the body bag? Pete was in "half" uniform and it would not be readily apparent that he was a police officer. "Oh boy" I thought "the shit really is going to hit the fan if he is injured as his rostered duty was control room operator!"

"642, one under arrest!" came the breathless report from Tommy. He would have had to reach the estate side of the underpass, and then run under the railway to get to Pete, and then deal with whatever he had found at the other end.

"Confirm it is the suspect from the robbery?" I asked.

"10/4" replied Tommy.

It occurred to me that there were no marked police vehicles at the scene of the arrest, as Pete had been in his own car and the others had been abandoned at the other side of the tracks. There was also going to be a possible conflict of interests as the arresting officer had also been at the scene, so contamination of forensic clues could be a problem.

"Control to Chief Inspector" I called. "We have one under arrest at Hunters Walk. Can you still attend for transport please?" as I knew he would not have had time to get there just yet.

"10/4 "replied Jim with obvious relief in his voice.

"All units, suspect from the robbery in custody, well done lads, thanks very much!"

"Wow" I thought as I looked at the clock "twenty two minutes from alarm to arrest, now that must be a record!"

I called Pete to confirm he was OK, and did they still need the dog section?

"Just checking" replied Pete.

"All is good; we've got the bag with the gun, the money and a knife, so nothing is outstanding."

I cancelled the dog section request, but SOCO would still attend to document the scene in case of future need.

At the same time I advised Force control that no other assistance was required, as they had been on standby to arrange out of town road checks and possible interception outside the divisional or force area. The firearms unit had been put on standby and could be stood down.

As a couple of other smaller jobs had come in and been put on hold I allocated officers to deal, and set about getting the incident report updated on the computer.

After a while the prisoner and escorts arrived, and as he was being dealt with a breathless Pete arrived in the office, a bit muddied and ruffled with a beaming smile on his face. He was babbling like a little school kid as he was telling anyone and everyone what had happened.

"I went to the top of Hunters Walk and parked up in my car" he said. "I hadn't been there long when I saw this guy coming through the underpass. It was getting dark so I couldn't really see him properly until he came under the streetlamp. I could see he answered the description, but was carrying a rucksack. Not many people go out jogging carrying a bag I thought to myself, so it was a little confusing. I got out and approached him, and of course he didn't seem too bothered 'cos I was in civvies."

"It was only when I got up close I saw something glisten on his trouser leg in the streetlight, and then I realised he was bleeding. I identified myself as a copper and he made as if to run off. I grabbed him and tripped him, but as we fell to the ground his bag jerked sideways and I saw the blade of a knife come through the side."

Oh Boy, if ever there was anything to get more adrenaline flowing I don't know what it could be.

"I radioed for help and clung on to him, trying not to let him get to his bag. Fortunately young Tommy seemed to arrive quickly and we got him cuffed. With the blood Tommy thought I was cut, but it was all from him as he had cut himself going through the glass door. Tommy says the assistant said the door had not even been locked, so it gave her chance to hit the panic buttons."

"Well done Pete" came the booming voice of Chief Inspector Jim Donaldson, "great result and all on your shift."

He said this just as a few members of the night shift were arriving and wondering what all the excitement was all about. And how come Pete had been involved?

As I was thinking I needed to get the job ready for nightshift, I threw in as an aside,

"What was the result at the insecure car repair place Pete?"

"Oh my gawd" gasped Pete, "Boss, can I have your car keys quick". As Pete had to escort the prisoner his own car was still up on Hunters Walk where he had left it. They all stared in amazement as Pete raced outside into the yard, blue lights on and away as fast as he could.

In a few minutes we heard Pete call in on the radio "I'm with the owner now, nothing missing and premises now secured. I'll explain the rest when I get back"

As the routine banter went on and the stories were being told from differing angles, a weary Pete arrived back looking a bit sheepish. Jim Donaldson looked a bit concerned as he asked Pete if everything was OK.

"Hopefully it is now, but don't be surprised if you don't get a complaint in the morning! I was at the insecure garage when the shout went up for the robbery. When Tom asked me to go to Hunters Walk, there was a lady walking past with a big Alsatian dog."

"I told her who I was, why I was there and that the key holder was on his way, and as I had been called away on a very very urgent police matter, would she mind terribly standing there until the key holder arrived or I came back. I didn't really give her much option and jumped in my car and raced off."

"Obviously with all the excitement I forgot all about her. It turns out the key holder only just arrived when I did. When I apologised profusely and told her I had just caught a robber, she put her nose in the air, huffed and said "a likely story if ever I heard one, when do we ever get robberies in this town?" and she strutted off. I haven't a clue who she was!"

The irony of the whole story was that "technically" Pete should never have been there. The reports were doctored so that Tommy McFarlane was shown as the arresting officer and no accolades or awards could be directed towards Pete without opening up a whole can of worms. So much for a quiet meal relief!

Chapter Twenty Two

Whenever a policeman appears on your doorstep, people automatically assume that they have either done something wrong or it is bad news. And they are normally right!

My duty was working a half night shift, meaning I was scheduled to work from six in the evening until two the following morning. I was on a foot beat, but was looking forward to completing a few follow up enquiries as it was generally easier to catch people in during the evening.

I had been making good progress when I received a radio message. Unfortunately it was to deliver a death message to one of the hundreds of holiday makers in the town. I was given an address which I knew to be in an area of rented holiday cottages, and because of the time I was probably going to find the person at home having something to eat.

All I had was the name of a female, and the message that her father had died suddenly.

I really didn't know who or what to expect. Some people accepted such news calmly, whereas others could become hysterical. There was however one golden rule which had been drilled into every police recruit at training, always, but always, confirm that the person you were talking to was the correct one!

I felt a shiver run down my spine as I recalled my first death message delivery.

I had been in company of my tutor constable, a not very able policemen, the type we referred to as a uniform carrier, who did the very minimum to earn his wage. We had been given an address which was in a small block of flats. As it happened there had been three blocks all identical next to each other.

As I had been a bit apprehensive and concentrating on exactly what I should say, I didn't really pay attention and just followed my tutor constable to the doorway of number seventeen.

A deep breath, loud knock and a young lady answered the door. The sight of a policeman at the door made her step back and her eyes went wide with trepidation. The message was regarding a young male who had been killed in a car crash earlier in the day, so it appeared to tie in with the information.

Fortunately, remembering my training, I asked politely,

"Hello, are you Susan Cooper?"

"Erm, no, I'm not" she replied somewhat confused.

"Is she in?" I continued.

"I'm sorry but there is nobody here by that name. We've lived here 15 years and don't know anyone called that."

I fumbled with my notebook, checking the address.

"This is 17 Barkers Court isn't it?" I asked tentatively.

A huge sigh of relief came from the young woman.

"No, no, you've got the wrong block! This is Barkers Grange. You need that one over there" she said, pointing across the way.

I quickly made my apologies and hurried away in embarrassment. After every interaction it was usual practice to discuss how things went with the tutor. It was very evident that things had gone wrong. I could see straight away that I had relied on the tutor to take me to the correct address.

You would think by now I should have learned not to trust this man's abilities, but that was no excuse for the error. Thank goodness I had checked the name.

There was an old joke at training school about delivering death messages.

Knock knock on the door, lady answers, "Are you the widow Brown?"

"No my husband is alive."

"Not anymore!"

Boom boom.

I had quickly confirmed the correct address and delivered the message but had never forgotten the lesson.

After a bit of a search I found the address I was looking for, definitely the correct one as it was a cottage with the wonderful name "Dunrovin," probably named originally as a retirement cottage by one of the seafarers in the area.

I rapped on the door with my usual "coppers knock."

There was call from inside "Just a minute" as a figure shuffled to the door.

When the door opened I could see a frail woman around forty five years old standing on crutches.

Upon seeing me standing there, her hand shot to her mouth and shrieked,

"Oh my God, it's my father isn't it?"

With that her knees appeared to give way and I caught her before she fell completely.

I had not said a word!!! But I had not yet had chance to check the golden rule.

"Is it Linda, Linda Castle?" I asked gently.

The response was a loud wail and massive sobs, I didn't need an answer. I desperately looked around to see if there was anyone else in the cottage. She appeared to be there by herself. I led her to one of the comfy chairs but as she sat down she started gasping for breath.

Real tortured gasping with a heavy wheezing sound, I realised she was probably asthmatic. Although I asked if she had an inhaler she was too shocked to answer, I frantically looked round the small room diner /kitchenette. I saw her bag on the window ledge and quickly located an inhaler and dashed back to where she was sitting.

She was really struggling to breathe; even as she took the inhaler I could see wild panic in her eyes, absolute terror. I waited an agonising couple of minutes to see if the inhaler would have any effect, but to my increasing frustration I saw the colour drain from her face and her lips had a bluish tinge developing.

She then slumped in the chair. I didn't know if she had fainted or worse, I quickly laid her on the floor in the recovery position, checking that she was breathing albeit very shallowly and then urgently radioed for an ambulance.

"What the hell just happened?" I thought to myself.

I quickly checked the rest of the cottage, definitely nobody there and no signs of a second occupant either. The keys were still in the lock on the inside so that would not be a problem as we left to go to hospital. I took a quick look in her handbag and located a driving licence. Sure enough, this was indeed Linda Castle.

After taking details of her home address I heard the ambulance coming, and as always went out to direct them in, I knew how frustrating it was trying to find the correct address in a hurry. I noted a small red car parked nearby with a disabled badge showing and guessed this might be hers.

The ambulance crew checked her over and put a mask on her face as they stretchered her outside. With remarkable foresight I remembered to take her handbag and her crutches out to the ambulance before locking the door and jumping into the ambulance myself.

Technically I still hadn't delivered the message! It was only a short trip to the hospital but the ambulance crew were still concerned for her wellbeing. She was obviously not a strong woman and not in good health.

I followed the crew into the emergency department and gave what details I knew to the duty sister. I knew better than to get in their way and went off to find the vending machine.

As I was just taking my first sip of tea, a woman I knew came into the department with an horrendous black eye and swollen bleeding lip.

She was the partner and punch bag of one of the nastiest men in town. He was a small wiry cocky little shit at the best of times. She was a petite blonde who, once linked with him could never escape his clutches. It didn't take too many guesses just who had inflicted those injuries, but I knew better to expect any complaint.

Sue Todd glanced at me but quickly looked away as she went to seek treatment.

"One day, just one day he would get his comeuppance" I thought. I had had dealings with the husband Paul "Sniffer" Todd on many occasions.

The duty doctor came across to me to explain that Linda would need to stay in for observation. I was concerned that the message had not been passed but realised she was not in any condition to receive the news, although she probably knew. The doctor said he would make sure the message was passed at a more suitable time. I made sure that they were aware of her possessions and crutches and felt I was no longer needed.

As I left I saw Sue sitting in the waiting area. I considered saying something, but knew that it would fall on deaf ears. I finished my cuppa and returned to the station.

I now needed to find out the origin of the death message and let them know of the problems I had encountered, and the fact that Linda was now in hospital and unlikely to be contacting them in the immediate future. Talk about rubbing salt in their wounds!

After I contacted the family I found out that the death of her father had not come totally out of the blue as the telex message had said, but as I had witnessed, Linda was not a strong woman and somewhat excitable. I was thanked for my efforts and they put the phone down.

My break time was due so I took the chance to take the weight off my feet. As I was just settling down my radio burst into life.

"I'd swear they have a camera in here" I thought. There was a domestic argument reported on my beat. I knew the address but it was a good fifteen minutes walk so I called for a lift from Pete in the van, and anyway the moral support would be welcomed.

Of course! It was Thursday, Giro day. That meant the ones on benefits who chose to spend their money on booze now had a free for all. It was often the case that it was not just the man about the house who would have a drink, but often the woman too, so they both became as bad as each other.

Some chose to shout. Some chose to throw things. Some chose to fight. I often felt sorry for the poor kids involved in those types of relationships; they would grow up and do exactly the same because they would know no better.

The problem with the domestics was that the arrival of the police often inflamed the situation. Sometimes it was the neighbours calling with concern for the battered wife or children; sometimes it was the battered wives calling. In the majority of cases, despite some awful injuries, charges were dropped the following day as complaint statements were withdrawn after they had kissed and made up (or the bully had threatened more violence.)

I knew from previous experience that this address was an unusual case. Yes they will both have been drinking. But, although the man became verbally abusive and loud he never used violence towards the woman. She, on the other hand, had been known to throw things, kick and pull hair. Meanwhile the kids looked on.

As the van pulled up outside the house, we could hear the shouting straight away. There were a few neighbours standing around, not sure if they were concerned or just watching for amusement.

Pete rapped loudly on the door which was quickly opened by a little five year old girl in pyjamas with a tear stained face. Somehow I felt this was not the first time she had done this.

The shouting continued from the living room and a sudden crash as something was broken. I stepped inside and moved to the source of the sound. I was just in time to see Karen Wilson launch another figurine in the direction of a cringing Bobby Wilson crouching in the corner.

"Who let you in?" she snarled, obviously just realising we were there.

"That doesn't matter" I said brusquely. "What does matter is that this needs to stop right now."

"Nobody asked you to interfere" she snapped.

"On the contrary, somebody was concerned enough to call us."

I looked over in the direction of Bobby, a broken man doing his best to live in the only world he knew.

From previous dealings, I knew Bobby was not a violent man. I also knew he worshipped the ground Karen walked on. She was definitely the bully in this relationship. As I expected they both smelled of alcohol.

I also knew that Bobby would do anything to keep the peace. One time after he had been reported missing, I had found him sleeping in the garden shed!

Whatever question I attempted to ask Bobby, Karen would answer for him. She was very upset over something or other but I couldn't determine exactly what, she seemed to twist the circumstances every few sentences.

Although she was definitely the aggressor, I had to consider the repercussions if we were to attempt to arrest her to prevent a breach of the peace. There was no way she was going to calm down. The children would be more upset seeing Mum carted off and she would then become more agitated (if that was possible).

I also knew that once Karen had chance to cool down a bit, she did become reasonable, but we didn't have time to sit and babysit the two of them.

"Is there anyone you can go stay with for the night?" I asked Bobby.

"He's not getting the family involved" hissed Karen immediately, as Bobby shook his head in resignation.

"Well, if you can't promise me that this isn't going to flare up again, then Bobby needs to come with us." I said, glancing towards the hang dog expression on Bobby's face.

You could virtually see the pleading in his eyes to get him out of there, tempered with the knowledge that he couldn't stand up to the woman in his life.

"If he thinks that he needs to hide behind your apron strings then God help us" she sneered.

You could hear the disgust in her voice and I sensed that the minute we left everything would erupt again if Bobby were to remain. I could see this would just go round and round so needed to be decisive.

"Right, Bobby is coming with us to prevent a further breach of the peace. He will be released in the morning without charge. Give the kids a chance to get to sleep and get some sleep yourself."

With that I led Bobby out into the hallway, allowing him to stoop down for a quick cuddle with the three bewildered wide eyed kids.

As we led him up the garden path Karen stood with the kids in the doorway. She spotted the group of neighbours huddled nearby,

"What are you lot gawping at?" she shouted before slamming the door.

It just goes to show how the law can be bent to suit the facts. I knew Bobby did not have the money to stay at a hotel, but felt it a bit ridiculous to provide nothing more than a free room for the night. If that kept the peace, so be it. We got a sheepish yet thankful Bobby back to the station and did the paperwork.

The rest of the shift had passed with the usual calls but nothing exceptional.

I returned to the station twenty minutes before the end of the shift to tie up some loose ends on paperwork, everything was quiet in the town as a light rainfall had cleared the streets quickly.

I then heard the three nines telephone ringing in the control room. I stopped putting my gear away and waited.

"688—Can you attend a domestic at 41 Benson Road" came the radio instruction.

The hairs instantly came up on the back of my neck. That address was very well known.

It just happened to be the residence of Sue and Paul Todd and family.

WPC688 Kath Montgomery was the area car driver. I immediately grabbed my jacket and radioed for her to pick me up for support as she had just driven into the rear yard anticipating going off shift.

Because it had come in on the three nines system from the actual address it sounded serious. Control reported it as a distressed female caller. As we arrived we could see two female figures at the doorway. I immediately recognised one as being Sue but didn't recognise the other one.

When we entered the doorway we could see blood spattered on the wall, and a closer look at the other female I could see blood smears around her nose and mouth.

Both of them were tearful with no sign of Paul.

It turned out that the other woman was Sue's sister.

"I don't care, you have to live with him, but I don't" she sobbed to her sister, "he's really gone too far this time and I want to press charges."

Sue was often an equal match in temperament to Paul, but when he had been drinking he became unpredictable. I could see the black eye and still swollen lip with what appeared to be a couple of stitches from earlier in the day. Both the "ladies" had been drinking.

"Where is he now?" Kath asked. We were both surprised to see them both nod towards the living room, thinking that he would have done a runner before we arrived. "And you are sure you want to press charges?" she confirmed with the sister.

"Yes, definitely!" she said.

"Please don't" pleaded Sue, "give him a chance."

"I did that last time! Now look what has happened" she sobbed.

As Kath was the dealing officer she went in first. Ironically she was the same size as Paul Todd, but I knew from previous experience that he was a real handful.

Paul was stretched out on the settee, his hands behind his head, looking calm and collected.

"Piss off out of my house" he hissed.

"You are under arrest for assault" Kath said as she continued to caution him. Paul sprang to his feet and stood in an aggressive stance.

"C'mon then, you try it" he goaded.

I stepped forward and tried to get hold of an arm but he was quick to dodge and ducked into the kitchen. As we followed him through I saw with dismay that there was a breadknife lying on the work surface surrounded by breadcrumbs. I knew Paul would not think twice to pick it up.

As I lunged forward using all my body weight to pin Paul against the wall, Kath managed to get a handcuff on one arm, but just as we were trying to get his second arm cuffed I felt a dull thump on the back of my head.

Sue had decided to come to the rescue of her husband and hit me with the frying pan! Not quite realising what was happening I pushed on to get the second cuff on. As soon as it was on Kath turned to wrestle the frying pan from a now screaming Sue.

Straight away Kath turned to her and told her she was under arrest for assault. As I realised things were likely to get out of hand I called for the van. I turned to Paul to move him to the door, unaware that I was slightly dizzy.

As I approached Paul the last thing I expected was the vicious head butt which connected with a loud thwack on the bridge of my nose.

Immediately blood poured from a cut above my nose and one nostril. I literally saw red, grabbed Paul by his hair and dragged him kicking and screaming outside.

The three women seemed to all stop what they were doing, they realised that the softly softly approach was finished.

Kath quickly cuffed Sue's arms behind her back; she also became aware of a small child trying to cling to her mummy's leg.

"Get that child out of here" she snapped to Sues' sister.

The sister seemed shocked and immediately grabbed the child as Kath grabbed Sue and dragged her outside.

The rain has started falling again outside as I pinned Paul down on the flagged area at the front of the house. I was actually dripping blood onto Paul and feeling dizzy. As the van arrived Paul started kicking out again.

As Pete jumped out of the van, one look at me instantly blew any idea of taking things easy. He opened the van doors and we literally threw Paul in. I was in no fit state to stay in the back with him. We decided that I would accompany Kath back to the station in the car with Sue and follow the van. We could see Paul kicking against the doors and windows.

"Now do you see why we called you?" Sue said. "He really has lost it today."

"What about you, why did you decide to have a go?" I said trying to stem the bleeding from my injured nose.

"Don't you see? I had to show him I was sticking up for him, otherwise when he gets home he will give me what for." She whimpered.

"I guess there is some sort of logic there," I acknowledged, my voice muffled with a rapidly increasing blood soaked handkerchief.

"I don't think he will be home for a while" hissed Kath as she took a pitiful look at my face, "assaulting your sister may be one thing, but assaulting police is something else."

Unfortunately I knew it would be another badge of honour for Paul even if he did get banged up for it.

They got Paul documented and into a cell so that I could get my injuries looked at. Kath was left to sort out Sue as I headed to hospital where A&E was empty and was soon being sorted out. I had a broken nose and three stitches to the bridge of my nose. My head was throbbing and I accepted some painkillers against my better nature.

Arriving back at the station, the duty sergeant who had expected to be going home early grimaced as he saw the state of me, the blood soaked shirt and dried blood around my face. He ordered me to go home, the others would deal with the paperwork, and I could do my statement later as Kath would be able to fill in any blanks.

What galled me most, had I not been hit by the frying pan I would have had my wits about me and more than likely avoided the head butt. Although I felt sorry for Sue, she really had been the deciding factor in the assault and would have to be brought to justice.

I also wanted to make sure someone got to the sister to get the promised statement of complaint as soon as possible. Without that the whole case would become diluted, where their defence would argue police harassment and that he was defending his home or whatever story they could cook up.

"Don't worry, we'll stitch him up good and proper" said Kath. "He'll get the message."

After the swelling went down the following week I still had trouble breathing through my nose. Several visits to the doctor and then a consultant ENT specialist revealed my right nostril was almost completely blocked and would remain so. The only way to correct it would be to re break my nose and reset it.

I really couldn't face that so learned to live with it. A subsequent health assessment listed me as having a two per cent disability for life! Wilson got three months for his antics but also a lifelong intolerance from the rest of my colleagues, nobody took any crap and he frequently got locked up using zero tolerance.

Sue managed to wriggle at court and got nothing more than slapped wrists. Last time I saw them both, they were hand in hand, staggering down the street on a drunken night out. Some people were made for each other